MW01087376

A Murder Down Memory Lane

A Myrtle Clover Cozy Mystery, Volume 26

Elizabeth Spann Craig

Published by Elizabeth Spann Craig, 2025.

This is a work of fiction. Similarities to real people, places, or events are entirely coincidental.

A MURDER DOWN MEMORY LANE

First edition. April 15, 2025.

ISBN: 978-1955395526

Written by Elizabeth Spann Craig.

Chapter One

"Seventy-five," said Myrtle with great conviction.

She and her friend Miles were sitting in rocking chairs on Myrtle's dock. It was July, there was a light breeze and shade from an oak tree to offer relief from the heat, and they were counting the number of songs a nearby mockingbird knew. Myrtle's feral cat, Pasha, looked out over the lake with interest, her tail swishing from time to time.

Miles, however, disagreed with Myrtle's count. "No, the bird clearly started over again around fifty-five. The rest were repeats that you didn't recognize as repeats."

Myrtle gave him a stern look. "I'm quite certain he didn't repeat any songs at all. They were all original." She rocked vigorously in her rocking chair.

Miles gave her a leery look. "Don't rock so violently. You ended up in the lake that one time."

"Which, as you know, had absolutely nothing to do with me and everything to do with a murderer who was trying to off me."

This minor argument might have continued for some time if Myrtle's phone hadn't trilled at her.

She frowned as she looked at the screen. "It's Sloan."

1

Sloan was the editor of the local paper, where Myrtle wrote a regular column and as many crime-related stories as she could get away with. "I wonder what he wants," she muttered.

"There's a good way to find out," suggested Miles helpfully.

The mockingbird continued his aria of songs in his repertoire as Myrtle answered the phone. Pasha looked longingly at the bird as if it appeared very tasty to her.

"Sloan," Myrtle said briskly. "How are things?"

Sloan stuttered a response. Myrtle had taught him English many years ago, and he always seemed to lose his ability to speak it properly when he was speaking with her. It always amazed her how he reverted right back to high school.

"Things are good," he said after a couple of moments. Then he seemed to get back into the swing of things.

"You're not calling me about that helpful hints column, are you?" she asked suspiciously. "I sent it in last week and it's nowhere close to being due again. No one needs *that* amount of helpful hints in their lives."

"No, no," said Sloan quickly. Myrtle could just imagine him perspiring in the newspaper office downtown as he attempted to find the words to express himself with Myrtle. "This call isn't about the column at all. I had a different idea for an assignment for you."

Myrtle bit back a sigh. So often, she had her hopes raised and dashed when Sloan offered her a story opportunity. She'd hope it would be an investigation of potential fraud or some other crime. But it would be a puff piece on someone turning one-hundred. As if that was some sort of remarkable accomplishment.

She was glad she hadn't hoped for much when Sloan said, "I believe your high school class is having a reunion tonight at the school. I was wondering if you could cover it for the paper. You know, quotes and so forth. A bit of description of the proceedings."

Myrtle glowered. "I know nothing about a high school reunion. Are you quite certain it's mine? Surely it's some other class reunion."

Now Sloan sounded even more nervous than he had previously. "Uh, I'm pretty sure, Miss Myrtle. I ran it by Red first, and he told me it was definitely your class."

Myrtle's brows knit in annoyance. "No one has contacted me regarding it. And everyone knows where I live. It's not as if I've moved for the last sixty or more years."

"Maybe the invitation got lost in the mail?" offered Sloan in a small voice. He clearly hoped Myrtle wouldn't take out her lack of inclusion on him, as the bearer of bad news. "Perhaps you should contact the class president. Isn't it usually the class president who organizes such things? If you remember who the class president was."

"Of *course* I remember who the class president was."

Sloan quickly said, "Right, right, of course you do. Although it would be understandable if you didn't. After all, it wasn't yesterday."

"No, you're quite right," said Myrtle coldly. "It was more like sixty-seven years ago. Which seems a very odd time to be having a class reunion. But, just the same, I'll cover the event for you." She paused. "Thanks, Sloan."

Now Sloan sounded vastly relieved as the uncomfortable conversation appeared to be drawing to a close. "Thanks to *you*, Miz Myrtle." He quickly hung up.

Miles was watching her with a quirked eyebrow. "I think you enjoy alarming Sloan."

"I consider it revenge for all Sloan's ineptitude in high school. And it's especially annoying that he had the impudence to become editor of a newspaper."

Miles said, "What was all that about a reunion?"

"That's what I'd like to know."

Pasha abandoned her fruitless interest in the mockingbird and jumped into Myrtle's lap. This had the intended effect of keeping Myrtle from the vigorous rocking that was threatening to toss her into the lake.

"You didn't receive an invitation?" asked Miles.

"Decidedly not. And I don't believe it was lost in the mail, as Sloan suggested. I think it must have been a deliberate snub." Myrtle looked quite aggravated.

Miles said slowly, "Do you know who might have organized a class reunion?"

"It would have to be Belinda Holloway. So very annoying."

"Annoying that she didn't invite you?" asked Miles.

"Annoying that she exists," said Myrtle. "At any rate, I'll be attending the reunion, anyway. Sloan just asked me to cover it for the paper."

"So you'll call Belinda Holloway."

"Certainly not," said Myrtle disdainfully. "I'll just crash the event."

Miles gave a shudder, the mere thought of party-crashing clearly occupying a prime spot in his catalog of personal terrors.

Myrtle looked at him in a considering fashion. "You could come as my plus-one."

"You don't have a plus-one. You weren't invited."

Myrtle conveniently ignored this interjection. "I'd imagine most of the guests will be there with a significant other."

"Surely that's unlikely, statistically speaking." Myrtle gave him a dark look, and Miles quickly attempted to redeem himself. "I mean, many people have lost a spouse. It's natural." But he was clearly just digging the hole deeper.

Fortunately, Myrtle, after shooting Miles another look, was willing to move on with the topic at hand. "Anyway, I'll just get the reunion details from Sloan, since he clearly has them. Then we'll go to the event."

Miles shook his head. "You're on your own, Myrtle. I'm absolutely not going to crash a party with you. It will not happen. You can go, catch up with your classmate chums, and report on the reunion. Then you can tell me all about it later."

Myrtle looked for a moment like she might argue the point before giving a shrug. "I suppose that's fine. Reunions aren't particularly fun anyway, are they?"

"Is there anyone in particular you'd be interested in seeing? This Belinda Holloway?" Miles hid a smile. Since Myrtle had described Belinda as annoying, he supposed she wasn't on Myrtle's list of favorite people.

Myrtle considered the question. "Honestly, I'm not sure how many alums will be there."

Miles supposed this meant that many of the alums might not be active anymore, but he was wise enough not to ask.

"Do you have a high school yearbook?"

"Naturally. Let's go inside, and I'll grab it."

Myrtle, being Myrtle, went right to it on the shelf. It had a green cloth cover and *Bradley High School* emblazoned on the front cover. She handed it to Miles, who handled the old volume gingerly.

"You had boys and girls at the same school?" Miles asked in surprise. "That must have been rather unusual at the time. In the South, I mean."

"It solved a budgeting problem for Bradley and made them look progressive," said Myrtle, shrugging.

Miles carefully turned the yellowed pages until he found Myrtle. She had a severe expression on her face, as if the photographer had somehow displeased her.

"A very attractive photo," said Miles politely.

Myrtle shrugged again. "I was too tall and my bones were too big. But I wasn't terrible."

Miles found a group photo further into the yearbook. It was the journalism club. Myrtle, at nearly six feet, towered over the girls and most of the boys. Again, she glowered at the camera.

"You didn't seem to be very fond of having your picture taken," noted Miles.

"The photographer was always saying ridiculous things to make us smile. I didn't appreciate it." Myrtle took the yearbook back from Miles. Flipping through the pages a lot rougher than he had, she frowned as she peered at various photos. She finally stopped at one, studying the faces. Then she thrust the book back at Miles.

He pushed his glasses up his nose, studying the page. It was a picture of the student government leadership. Miles spotted the name "Belinda" under one picture. She was a stunning blonde with a megawatt smile and perfect posture. Belinda seemed also to be dressed in the height of fashion. Myrtle, as the student government secretary, looked perfectly tidy in a dress that Miles suspected her mother might have made.

"I'm guessing Belinda might have been a bit much," said Miles diplomatically.

Myrtle snorted. "In every way. Since she was the class president, she'd have been the one tasked with organizing the reunions." She frowned. "Since I have no information on this event, I'm going to have to call Sloan back."

Miles hid a smile as Sloan nervously dropped something on his end of the phone when Myrtle called him back. He wouldn't have known Myrtle was aggravated at Belinda for not inviting her, and not at Sloan. A minute later, she had all the information she needed. Judging from her expression, it hadn't made her happy.

"The reunion is tonight," she said with displeasure. "Now I'll have to put my funeral dress on. I haven't taken a proper look at my funeral dress for a while. It might need attention." Myrtle's funeral dress had developed the uncanny ability to collect stains and crumbs during its time in her closet, as if it moonlighted at dinner parties while she slept.

Miles said, "I thought you had purchased some other funeral garments."

"Yes, a nice pant suit-type thing. But I'm not at all sure that's suitable for crashing reunions. I likely haven't seen some of these people in quite a while. I should look nice."

Miles said, "Maybe you should take a look at the dress now, while it's daylight outside. Then you can see if it will work."

Myrtle was already halfway to her bedroom by the time Miles had finished speaking. She came out with a somber-looking dress on a hanger. They scrutinized it as Myrtle held it in a sunbeam coming in from the living room window.

"I think it looks perfectly respectable," said Miles.

Myrtle made a face. "I'm not sure respectable was the look I wanted."

"You could liven it up a little with a scarf or some jewelry," suggested Miles.

"The only scarves I have are the winter kind. And my jewelry is all cheap and costume."

Miles gave Myrtle a curious look. "You aren't trying to outshine Belinda, are you?"

"What? No. But I have to look professional and appropriate, of course. Considering I'm representing the local newspaper." She frowned at Miles. "Are you sure you won't come?"

"Absolutely."

"All right then," said Myrtle crossly. "I suppose I'll go myself."

"You wouldn't be nervous about crashing the reunion, I suppose."

"Certainly not," said Myrtle, gritting her teeth. "I'll enjoy every moment."

Chapter Two

As a matter of fact, Myrtle did enjoy crashing the reunion at her high school. For one thing, she simply enjoyed being back at the old school. She might not have enjoyed her years as a student there, but she'd enjoyed most days as a teacher. Aside from dealing with school administrators and endless staff meetings, of course. Those had been tiresome. There were a couple of principals who just enjoyed hearing the sound of their own voices.

As Myrtle had expected, there were not many vehicles in the parking lot in front of the school. But then, she herself hadn't parked a car there, either. Elaine, her lovely daughter-in-law, had come in her minivan full of scattered Cheerios cereal detritus and Myrtle's grandson, Jack, to drive her to the school.

Elaine pulled in front of the school. "Is it good to be back?" she asked.

"It's a little strange," said Myrtle. "I spent so many years here, teaching. That building has had a lot of renovation, though, since my time."

"I bet it looks different," said Elaine.

"It's both very familiar and very strange. Like visiting an old friend who's had extensive plastic surgery."

The bones of the brick building were the same with the imposing stone steps and the tall windows that had witnessed many decades of teen drama. Now the entrance sported an accessibility ramp, which had been sorely needed, even in Myrtle's day. Security cameras peered down from discreet corners as a modern necessity that Myrtle had never needed to consider.

"You look wonderful, Myrtle," said Elaine, giving her a warm smile. "Is that lipstick new?"

It was actually an ancient tube of lipstick, in a shade no longer being manufactured. But Elaine had probably never seen her wearing makeup. "It used to be new," said Myrtle. "Thanks for driving me here, Elaine. Red's picking me up, I think you said?"

"That's right. I'd come get you later, but I suspect I'll be in the middle of Jack's bath time then."

Jack blew Myrtle a kiss as she climbed out of the front seat of the van. She blew one back, then squared her shoulders and headed toward the school.

The heavy doors opened into the freshly waxed hallway that smelled exactly as it had during her teaching years—a peculiar mix of floor polish and adolescent anxiety. She saw motivational posters in place of the class photos that had once hung there, though she noticed they'd kept the old trophy cases. She paused in front of them, seeing trophies from her own high school days as well as more recent triumphs.

Signs with lots of exclamation points and decorated with balloons directed attendees to the gym where Myrtle could already hear muted conversation and what sounded like Glenn Miller being played at a sensible volume. Before heading in that direction, Myrtle couldn't resist pausing to see her old classroom.

She tried the door, somewhat surprised to find it locked. She peeked through the window instead. Myrtle frowned, seeing the blackboard had been replaced by some sort of digital whiteboard. She supposed it was progress of some sort, but doubted it would be as satisfying an experience as making a point on a blackboard with a stick of chalk.

As she walked through the gym, she suspected she was going to have to deal with a good amount of nonsense and foolishness. Streamers in the school's colors and balloons were in evidence, although there appeared to be punch and a nice spread of food. But then, Belinda wasn't one to take responsibility lightly.

Myrtle received some satisfaction as the attendees turned and looked in silence as she walked toward them, head held high in her funeral dress. Belinda looked rather taken aback as she stood by the punch bowl, elegant as always in what seemed to be expensive clothing.

"Myrtle," she said archly. "What a surprise."

"Yes, isn't it?" asked Myrtle in a sweet voice. "Sloan Jones, the editor of the local paper, was kind enough to ask me to write a story about our reunion. It seemed churlish of me to refuse him. He relies on me so much."

"You work for the paper?" asked Belinda.

Myrtle couldn't tell from her tone if she was intrigued or disgusted by the prospect of working. "That's correct. Of course, you wouldn't know that, having moved away." She pulled out a notebook and pen from her large purse. "I'm assuming you're the one who planned this shindig? And invited the others?" She cocked an eyebrow at Belinda. She certainly would not give the slightest indication that she'd felt slighted at being excluded.

It pleased her to see Belinda look uncomfortable. "Yes, I organized the event and invited others. Not inviting you was an oversight. I thought you'd . . . passed away."

"The reports of my death have been greatly exaggerated," said Myrtle sharply. "Which you could easily have found on social media. I maintain an online presence, you know."

"Do you? I'm afraid I don't. It always seemed so unnecessary and plebeian to me." Belinda gave a light laugh.

Myrtle was very surprised to hear such a limited take on social media. She jotted something down in her notebook while Belinda looked more uncomfortable than she had before.

Myrtle said, "I have to wonder what made you decide to have a reunion *this* year?" She studied Belinda's features as if looking for the truth in them.

"Well, we're not getting any younger, Myrtle. I thought it might be a case of now-or-never. Besides, I had time on my hands, which is not something I usually have. I'm always planning a family reunion or a bridge party or a church gathering. It's July, so school is out and it's easy to have access to Bradley High." She shrugged an elegant shoulder.

"But it's our 67th reunion. It's nothing remarkable."

"*Every* year is remarkable at our time of life!" said Belinda with a brittle laugh.

A voice came from behind them. "Sakes alive! Could it possibly be the fair maiden, Myrtle Clover?"

Myrtle froze. She had the horrible feeling that, when she turned around again, she'd face Winston Rouse. Belinda now had a smirk on her face, which Myrtle would very much like to wipe away.

There appeared to be no escape from Winston. He came around to face her and reached for her hand with both of his. He was wearing a festive red bow tie, a sports jacket, and had a neatly trimmed white beard. His eyes twinkled merrily at her. "What an extraordinary honor to have you here this evening, Myrtle!" He winked at her. Belinda's smirk grew larger and even more obnoxious than it had been before.

Myrtle was not happy to see Winston. When she'd last seen him, some time ago at Greener Pastures Retirement Home, he'd seemed in romantic pursuit of her. Winston had been flirtatious, charming, and quite complimentary of Myrtle when they'd been young. He'd been well-read and smart. These were all things that Myrtle had liked about Winston. She rarely admitted to herself that she had fallen for his flirtation at one time. However, the things Myrtle *disliked* about Winston soon outnumbered the positives.

"Hello, Winston," said Myrtle stiffly.

Winston was not to be deterred. "I've been trying to get somebody to dance with me since Belinda started up the Glenn Miller music. Would you like to trip the light fantastic?"

Myrtle lifted her cane at him, a gesture which came across as threatening rather than as an excuse for her reluctance to dance.

"I didn't mean trip in a literal way. I would never let you fall," declared Winston in his booming voice. "You'll be in safe hands."

Myrtle decidedly did not want to be in Winston's hands in any way. "Actually, I'm here to do some work for the paper, not to enjoy myself. I'm covering the event for the *Bradley Bugle*."

Winston sighed. "Well, that's a shame. Maybe another time." He looked hopefully at Belinda. "Would you like to go for a spin? You wouldn't turn me down, would you? You'll remember I'm still in touch with your sister. I'd like to tell her we shared a dance."

Belinda gave him a severe look. "I've already danced once. And I've got other things I need to do, since I'm in charge of the event. Myrtle, let me give you a tour of the different stations I've set up for the reunion. I'm sure the newspaper's readers will be interested in seeing photos of them."

Myrtle was relieved when Belinda whisked her away, although she was certain Belinda was less interested in saving her from Winston than she was in publicizing all her hard work for the reunion.

"These are stations I've set up. I thought it would be fun to have little triggers to help us reminisce about the old days."

There was a table set up with old yearbooks opened to their class, a table with loose photographs from their time at the school, and another with printed emails of the attendees' recollections from their schooldays.

Belinda was pulled away by Winston on some other pretense, affording Myrtle the opportunity to look around her for a few moments before taking photos. She found, to her amazement, that she recognized the other people at the reunion. As expected, there were only a handful.

Dr. Harold Blackwood stood with his wife, Evie. He was squinting at the photographs through his bifocals. Evie hovered nearby, occasionally touching his arm and seeming very solicitous of him. Myrtle had the feeling Dr. Blackwood might be a suitable target for a few quotes on the reunion.

Frank Lawson was peering into another trophy cabinet, this one in the back of the gym. He'd been quite the athlete in high school, remembered Myrtle. She suspected he might want to go on and on about his glory days, so perhaps he was not the best individual for good quotes. He brightened considerably as he spotted her, and she quickly pretended not to have seen him.

Millie Thatcher was studying the displays with poorly concealed disdain. Apparently, she was not a fan of Belinda's efforts. Myrtle remembered her as a slender, rather mousy girl who was always carrying an armload of books.

Gladys Pinkerton was also present. She'd been something of a follower in high school, trying to be part of the crowd. From what Myrtle could tell, she seemed to be doing the same thing now.

Myrtle walked over to the food table, or station, as Belinda had called the different tables. Belinda had borrowed the plastic trays from the cafeteria to evoke their schooldays, although Myrtle remembered the food back then had not remotely looked as good as the food here. There were pimento cheese sandwiches cut into triangles, ham salad sandwiches on white bread, cheese straws, deviled eggs, and a bowl of salted mixed nuts. On the sweeter side were lemon squares and pound cake slices. A punch bowl was nearby with what tasted like ginger ale and sherbet. Myrtle suspected the cost of attending the reunion was either very low, or Belinda had made all the food herself. She took a few cautious bites. It was actually all very good. Which irritated Myrtle even more.

By the time Belinda clapped her hands to get everyone's attention, Myrtle was seething with annoyance. Perhaps because, in *this* setting, which had been her workplace for decades, *she'd* been the one in charge. At least in her classroom.

Even more annoying, Belinda seemed to be proposing a game of some sort. "Everyone! I've come up with a fun activity for us all. A scavenger hunt."

The group murmured. It was hard to tell if the murmur was pleased or not.

Belinda apparently decided on the former. "Yes, won't it be fun? I thought we might all enjoy seeing how much things have changed since our own days at good old Bradley High." She turned to Evie. "Could you pass one of these cards to everyone?"

Evie did as instructed. Myrtle declined a card on the grounds that she was there to work. But she took a picture of one card with Evie smiling in the background. Looking at the photo, Myrtle spotted some scavenger hunt locations that made sense: the chemistry lab, their old homeroom. But others seemed oddly specific, like the art room (which hadn't been around when they were in school), and a particular corner of the library.

"The cards are all slightly different so we won't all be in the same locations at the same time. Let's all meet back here in thirty minutes," said Belinda, "so don't spend too long of a trip down memory lane! There'll be a prize for the winner." She looked around her. "And I might catch up with some of you individually as we scatter around. There are just so many happy memories to discuss."

The suggestion of wandering around the school seemed more popular with the group than the forced interaction in the gym had been. Their countenances had brightened considerably. Although Myrtle felt like she was back in high school. Gladys had immediately tried to attach herself to Belinda, who was still the popular girl, and had been rebuffed as Belinda linked her arm with Harold's. Harold's wife looked none too amused.

"I might take a look at the other trophy cases near the high school's entrance," announced Frank-the-former-athlete to the room, looking hopefully at Myrtle. Myrtle was in no mood to be impressed and pretended to be so absorbed by her phone that she hadn't heard him. It was a very odd situation, having the tables turned like this. Usually, the old women were chasing after the old men, since there was such a dearth of them.

Everyone headed out, cards in hand, for the scavenger hunt as Glen Miller's music followed them.

Myrtle had already seen most of what she'd wanted to see. Besides, she'd been at the school since retiring. She was a bit more curious about what Belinda was saying to Harold to make his face the scarlet shade it was turning. Harold's wife, Evie, walked up and tried to interrupt their conversation as Belinda waved her away dismissively. Belinda had said she wanted to catch up with former classmates individually, but she hadn't mentioned engaging in upsetting conversations.

No one was operating in groups, apparently preferring to work alone in order to win the prize. Myrtle waited in the gym for everyone's return. She'd finished taking her photos and had some more of those pimento cheese triangles. They were surprisingly good. She hadn't taken Belinda for someone who might be proficient in home skills.

Then Myrtle took a seat at a table to wait for the others. She might have dozed off because she was surprised when she heard voices returning and realized thirty minutes had already passed. To cover up the fact she'd been napping, she leaped to her feet to take pictures of the incoming reunion attendees. They all seemed quite chatty now, and were showing off their scavenger hunt cards to each other.

After Myrtle had taken a few pictures and gotten a couple of quotes from a grouchy Evie and an irrepressible Gladys, she noticed everyone seemed to be waiting for something. She frowned. "Where's Belinda?" Myrtle asked.

Everyone looked at each other and shrugged.

This was most irritating. Myrtle suspected Belinda was planning on making a grand entrance. She always was an attention hog. Myrtle wasn't in the mood to attend the reunion much longer. She'd already decided she'd leave after taking a picture of the winner of the scavenger hunt. "Harold," she said sharply. "You were the last one who saw her."

Harold frowned, and Evie said just as sharply, "He wasn't. Belinda was talking to others, too. I saw her speaking with Frank."

Frank shook his head quickly. "She didn't want to talk to me. Belinda was too busy trying to talk to Gladys."

Gladys turned a rosy shade of pink. "That was a quick conversation. Only a minute."

"Winston?" asked Myrtle.

Winston gave an apologetic shrug.

Millie, still looking disdainful, said, "We don't really need Belinda here, do we? I won the scavenger hunt—anyone can look at my card and see that."

Myrtle said in frustration, "Doesn't anyone know where the woman is? For heaven's sake. She's the one who's supposed to be in charge here."

They all looked at Myrtle as if waiting for her to fill in temporarily. She blew out a sigh. "Okay. I need to take pictures of the winner then call my son to pick me up. Who found all the items on the scavenger hunt? Millie, you mentioned you had."

Millie Thatcher raised her hand, always the perfect student.

Frank said, "I think we should find out who came in second place."

Myrtle said sternly, "As far as I'm aware, there was no mention of a second-place prize. So we'll forego that. Millie, stand over here and smile."

"Where's my prize?" demanded Millie, looking fractious.

"Who knows? I'm not the one who's supposed to be distributing prizes. Just hold out your winning scavenger hunt card."

Myrtle felt as if she were dealing with children instead of very senior citizens. She took the picture of a visibly tense Millie with the card, then pulled out her phone.

"Red? I'm ready to head out now."

Her son sounded very much as if he might be in the middle of his supper. "Right now? You sure weren't over there long, were you?"

Myrtle said, "About an hour. It was time enough." She didn't think she wanted to see any of her former classmates again.

Red sighed. "Okay. Let me swallow down this food, and I'll be right there."

Myrtle hung up. She found everyone was still staring at her as if she were the master of ceremonies. What was more, she couldn't decide what her gut was trying to tell her. Was she wanting more pimento cheese sandwich triangles? Or was she, perhaps, concerned about Belinda? Surely the woman couldn't have fallen and have a broken hip somewhere in the building, could she?

Myrtle decided Belinda couldn't. She seemed to be a very surefooted woman, even in the heels she was wearing. Even so, she couldn't seem to shake the feeling. She started heading for the gymnasium door.

"Where are you going, Myrtle?" asked Gladys.

"I'm just checking something," said Myrtle. "Continue with whatever you were all doing."

Which was nothing. A couple of them followed her, which was most annoying. It nearly made Myrtle make a sharp detour to the ladies' room, just to shake them.

Gladys was one of her followers. She stuck to her like a limpet. "Where are we going?" she asked breathlessly.

Winston was along for the ride, too. He was either trying to catch Myrtle on her own or Gladys. Both he and Gladys were chatting as they walked.

Myrtle peeked into the cafeteria (which looked startlingly different from the way it had when she'd been teaching, and absurdly different from when she'd been a student there), the library, and a couple of other spots on the scavenger hunt list. Then she wandered around, looking for the art room. There was no map and no signs on the walls, so wandering was definitely in order. Gladys and Winston were jabbering with each other and any interruption might redirect their attention toward her.

Finally, she spotted a door that had artwork on either side. Myrtle turned the door handle, pushed the door open, and walked inside.

There she found Belinda on the floor, dead.

Chapter Three

M yrtle stopped so abruptly that Gladys ran into her back, then Winston into Gladys's, pushing Myrtle forward until she used her cane to come fully upright again. "Back off," growled Myrtle.

"What's happening?" asked Gladys, trying to peer around Myrtle.

"Belinda is dead," said Myrtle in a clipped tone.

"*Dead*? But she can't be."

"Of course she can be. And she is," said Myrtle.

"Should I call the police?" asked Winston, the jocularity now missing from his voice.

Myrtle said absently, "The police are on their way." Of course, the police, represented by her son, Red, were going to be waiting outside the building for her to come out. But he'd eventually come inside, probably fairly aggravated at having to do so.

She turned around. "We need to protect the area. Winston and Gladys, back out of here. I'm going to ensure the crime scene is secured."

"Crime scene?" asked Winston.

"Indeed. It's very clear."

"Not a suicide then?" asked Winston.

"With a paint can?" Myrtle was losing her patience. But then, her patience had been in low supply since she'd first arrived at the reunion.

Gladys's voice quivered as she spoke. "Is she really dead? Shouldn't we try CPR or something?"

Myrtle had never believed Gladys to be the sharpest tool in the shed. "No, Gladys. Belinda is very dead, I'm afraid. Now you and Winston go back to the others. Tell them what happened and wait there." Her voice brooked no disagreement.

The two of them turned and left. Myrtle took several pictures with her phone. Not for the paper, of course, but for her own investigation. The paint can was the obvious weapon. It had clearly been swung with some force at Belinda. She was lying on her front, so whomever had done this had taken her by surprise.

The rest of the art room was undisturbed. Although there'd been no art room when Myrtle and the rest of them had been in high school, it had obviously been a staple for some time. The room smelled of tempera paint and clay dust. Large windows lined one wall, their blinds drawn for the night. Student artwork was strung on wire lines across the room, creating irregular shadows in the overhead light.

It was a backdrop for which Myrtle would never expect to find Belinda. And, considering how she'd always carried herself with such regal poise, it was quite disconcerting to see her crumpled on the floor near one of the pottery wheels. Her silver hair, so perfectly coiffed earlier, was now matted with blood and in disarray.

Myrtle glanced around to see if she could spot Belinda's cell phone. It would have been nice to pull tissues from her purse and carefully scroll through it, looking for clues as to why one of their classmates would kill her. Because it was completely obvious that's what had happened. One of these octogenarians had mustered enough strength and will to swing the paint can at Belinda's head. Myrtle would very much like to find out why. It was very interesting that Belinda had mentioned wanting to catch up with various attendees. She wondered if Belinda had some sort of ulterior motive.

Belinda's cell phone was nowhere in sight, but Myrtle's started bleating at her, which startled her. She grimaced. It was likely Red. He must have arrived at the school and wondered why she wasn't coming out. Knowing Red, he'd probably assumed she'd taken a tumble down one of the many staircases. He was always looking for an excuse to toss her into Greener Pastures Retirement Home.

Reluctantly, Myrtle pulled her phone out of her purse and backed out of the door, electing to stand directly outside the room as sentinel. Instead of texting Red back, she called him. "Red. There's been an incident."

"Don't tell me somebody slipped on those waxy floors. That high school is no place for a reunion. I don't know why they couldn't have planned it in a hotel's conference room like normal people," grouched Red.

"It's something more of an incident than that. You'll need to call the state police. The reunion's organizer has been murdered."

"What?"

"You heard me. And I suppose you'll want to come inside, too. Everyone else is supposed to be in the gymnasium, but the murder took place in the art room." Myrtle hung up as Red continued to splutter. She did hope he'd call that nice Lieutenant Perkins and tell him to come over and assist. Myrtle always did enjoy spending time with him.

A few minutes later, she heard Red barking commands to the others, presumably to get them out of the high school altogether, but staying on the campus until he could question them all. Then she heard some stomping around. "Mama?" he called, his voice sounding fairly strident.

"Here," she called back impatiently.

"I don't know where *here* is. Or the blasted art room."

"Just follow my voice," said Myrtle. "I'll sing a song."

Red said something that very much sounded like "please don't," and Myrtle starting singing *Mary had a Little Lamb* at high volume. It was funny how her voice warbled now. She didn't recall it being so quavery years ago.

"I'm here, I'm here," said Red quickly at the door. She was still standing there, right outside.

Myrtle gestured to Belinda's body within. Red gave her a curt nod. "Stand with the others outside. I take it you know who this woman is?"

"Certainly, I do. It's Belinda. We went to high school together." She paused. "Is the state police coming? I'd like to talk to Perkins."

"Yeah, they're on the way. Should be here shortly because they were working something in the area that's wrapping up. But

I don't think it's going to be Perkins. From what they told me, he's taking some well-deserved time off," said Red.

"That's most inconvenient."

Red pointedly ignored her as he starting stringing up crime scene tape. Myrtle got out of the way, thumping with her cane as she headed for the exit.

The others were grouped together out front. They looked up as she came out the door and gingerly made her way down the stairs.

"What happened?" demanded Millie.

Myrtle shrugged. "You probably know as much as I do. Belinda was walking around observing the scavenger hunt challenge. Someone murdered her in the art room, which was a location on the card. Didn't any of you see anything?"

Everyone looked at everyone else. They shook their heads.

Myrtle said impatiently, "Millie, as the winner of the hunt, surely you saw something. You must have been in the art room at some point."

Evie said loudly, "Harold and I couldn't even find the art room."

Millie was sullen. "I went to the art room first. Followed my nose there. You could smell the paints. When I was in there, there wasn't a dead body anywhere in sight." She stalked away and the others, aside from Gladys, walked over to stand with her and talk in hushed voices.

"Has it been long since you've seen Belinda?" Myrtle asked Gladys casually. "I mean, besides here at the reunion."

"Me? Mercy, no. She and I have been close friends for decades," said Gladys proudly before her face crumpled. "I can't believe this is happening."

Myrtle had an abhorrence for tears, so quickly moved to ask more questions and divert her from the emotional breakdown that seemed forthcoming. "You two lived in the same town, then, presumably? Where was that?"

"Atlanta," said Gladys simply.

"Goodness. The big city. That must have been quite a change from Bradley."

Gladys nodded. "It was, but in a good way. There was always something fun to do there. And people to watch. It can be fun people-watching, you know."

Myrtle nodded. People-watching was one of her own activities, too. However, Myrtle felt certain she might glean more from her study of human beings than Gladys did.

"You and Gladys were friends in high school, I believe," said Myrtle.

Gladys nodded happily. "The best of friends."

"You weren't on the cheerleading squad, though. Not like Belinda was."

Gladys gave a rueful chuckle. "Heavens, no. I've never been that coordinated. Not like that. Doing all those flips and things. I'd have broken my neck. Maybe if I could have cheered while wearing a helmet or something."

Myrtle thought that would have been quite a sight, especially back then. Nowadays, the calisthenics were so complex that a helmet was a smart idea, at least in Myrtle's way of thinking. "Were you and Belinda in similar fields?"

Gladys frowned. "Fields? Like corn fields?"

Myrtle managed to repress a sigh. "No, I meant were you in the same occupations?"

"Oh, I see. No, I was a secretary. I mean, assistant. Belinda went into real estate."

Myrtle was surprised. She hadn't thought Gladys bright enough to have a career whatsoever, and secretaries had to be sharp. She likely didn't have time to speak with Gladys on lighter topics, so she didn't ask any further personal questions. Red was almost certain to come back outside and ruin her opportunity to glean information.

"Thinking back to Belinda, did you see her during the scavenger hunt?"

Gladys's eyebrows drew together. "You already asked that when we were in the gym."

"I'm just trying to get an idea when she died and who might have seen something important. You never know—something you think is insignificant could be something very important."

Gladys looked doubtful. She said, "I spent some of the time during the game using the restroom. The rest of the time, I was looking for Belinda. I wanted to talk with her."

"Did you look in the locations listed in the hunt?"

"Sure, I did. But maybe she was in those locations at different times." Gladys shrugged. Then she looked mildly ill. "You don't think she was dead on the floor the whole time I was looking for her, do you?"

"That's what I'm trying to figure out. It would be nice to have a timeline. I'm sure that's what the police will be piecing together, too." Myrtle frowned at Gladys. "Was there a particular reason you were trying to find Belinda to begin with?"

Gladys pursed her lips together. "Well, it's something I'd rather not talk about. Something private."

"There's really no privacy when it comes to a murder investigation."

Gladys looked quite fierce now. "I don't want anything going in the newspaper."

"For heaven's sake, I'm not wanting to write an expose on you. Or on Belinda, for that matter. I'm simply trying to get to the truth."

Gladys still seemed somewhat suspicious, but finally reluctantly said, "I was hoping to talk with her about a business opportunity."

Myrtle frowned. "You're selling life insurance or something?"

"No, no, nothing like that." Gladys pressed her lips together as if determined nothing else would escape.

"I see. Well, maybe you can fill me in on Belinda. I haven't seen her for decades."

Gladys considered this. "Well, we were best friends, like I said. She and I had weekly lunch dates for over forty years. And, of course, she relied on me as a confidante. She was divorced twice, you see. Belinda needed someone to lean on. I even helped her with research for her real estate dealings." Gladys beamed.

"Well, that's all very nice," said Myrtle.

"Isn't it? I'll miss her terribly. We were to go on a cruise together this winter."

Myrtle asked, "How about you, Gladys? Do you have a family?"

Her expression grew cloudy. "No, I never married or had children of my own. I had lots of wonderful pets, though. They made my life feel very fulfilled. I spend a good deal of time volunteering at the animal shelter." Gladys flashed a quick smile at thinking of the animal shelter, and Myrtle had an equally quick glimpse at her teeth. Myrtle winced. It appeared Gladys might be in need of dental work.

Myrtle heard Red and glanced up in irritation. He was talking on his phone and glowering at Myrtle.

She quickly turned back to Gladys. "It sure looks like someone here at the reunion might have murdered Belinda."

Gladys blinked at her. "No. That can't be. Everyone was Belinda's friend."

"I'm afraid someone must not have been. Since you were so very close with Belinda, do you have any idea who that might be?"

But Gladys appeared stubbornly convinced it couldn't have been one of their former classmates. "Everyone loved Belinda."

"Right. But even people who love each other argue sometimes. Or disagree with one another. Did you see or hear anything this evening that might give us a clue?"

Gladys looked again as if she was going to automatically reject the idea once again. Then she paused. Her gaze rested on the group, still talking some distance away. "I did hear Evie and Belinda arguing at one point."

"What were they arguing about?"

Gladys sighed. "Oh, I don't know. It could have been anything, couldn't it? Maybe Evie didn't think the scavenger hunt was fair or maybe she thought Belinda hadn't done a good job organizing the reunion."

Myrtle very much doubted this was the case.

Red had unfortunately wrapped up his phone call and was now speaking in a raised voice. "Everyone, if I could have your attention. I need to make sure before you all leave the school grounds that you leave a statement and your contact information for the police. My deputy and the state police are on their way and should be here shortly. No one is allowed back inside the building. I'll also ask that you all stay in town until the investigation is further along."

There were groans and mutterings in response, which Red ignored. Myrtle glanced over at Gladys and saw her anxious look. She had the sudden certainty that Gladys was not in the best financial situation. Perhaps she'd intended to spend a single night at a local hotel instead of multiple nights. Myrtle did, of course, have a small guest room. However, she did not feel inclined to offer it to Gladys.

Red went back into the building, and the former classmates found places to either prop themselves up against a wall, or stairs to sit on. Myrtle decided just to lean on her cane. Gladys was still standing by her, looking concerned.

Gladys seemed in the mood to reminisce. "I did love my years at Bradley High," she said wistfully. "Life seemed so easy back then, didn't it?"

"Did it?" Myrtle felt as though adolescence was something of a jungle. One had to make one's way through it without much direction.

"It sure did. Think about it—we didn't have anything to worry about. Our parents looked after us."

Myrtle's memories weren't quite the same. "I remember worrying quite a lot about tests and projects. And college applications. My parents both worked, so I was also on the rotation for making supper." Although, in Myrtle's recollection, her rotation hadn't lasted long before her mother and father abruptly took it back over. Perhaps they were concerned about her taking too much time from her studies for cooking.

"Your mama worked, too?" Gladys's eyes were wide. "What did she do?"

"Oh, she taught. It was the family trade," said Myrtle with a shrug.

Gladys squinched up her face, apparently trying to dredge up a memory embedded deeply in her head. "Your daddy was the principal at Bradley High, wasn't he?"

"That's right. He'd taught for years, but then got pressured into administration."

"Did he like it?" asked Gladys.

"No, I think he loathed it. It's not why he went into education. He should have stayed in the classroom."

Gladys still had her rose-colored glasses on when it came to her high school days. "Still, they were such fun days. I loved hanging out with Belinda and the other cheerleaders, even though I wasn't in cheer. They were always so nice."

Myrtle had a different memory. She'd thought at the time that they treated Gladys like a lackey or a hanger-on.

"What group did you hang out with?" asked Gladys. "I don't remember you going to the football games and all." She squinched up her face again, still working on dredging those memories. "I don't even think I remember seeing you at lunch."

"I ate lunch in the journalism room. Those were the kids I associated with." It had been a motley assortment, but an amiable group.

A voice at Myrtle's elbow made her jump. It was Frank Lawson, apparently still on the make. "Are y'all doing okay?" he asked solicitously. "What an awful thing to happen."

Gladys teared up, which was definitely not what Myrtle wanted. She dug around for a packet of tissues and thrust them at the weeping Gladys while Frank patted her on the shoulder.

"Now, now," he said. "It's going to be okay."

It wasn't, of course. Not for Belinda, at any rate. Myrtle was about to turn her questioning on Frank when several police cars drove up to the school in rapid succession.

Chapter Four

"Here comes the cavalry," muttered Myrtle. It was most disappointing that Perkins was away. In his place seemed to be a dark-haired man with a thin mustache and a stern expression. He spoke briefly with Red, then turned to scrutinize the group. Spotting Myrtle, he gestured for her to come over.

Myrtle thought this rather rude. Surely, *he* should have been the one to walk over to *her*. Age has its privileges, after all, although they could be few and far between. Sullenly, she joined the officer.

He introduced himself as Detective Randall Shaw with the state police. "I've heard about you, Mrs. Clover."

Myrtle had the feeling he wasn't meaning that as a compliment. "Heard about me? In what regard?"

"I've heard you have a penchant for murder."

Myrtle raised her eyebrows. "I believe you don't know the definition of 'penchant.'"

This made the officer frown. "I mean that you are always around when murders take place."

"Perhaps you're looking for other words. It's a coincidence that I happen to be around shortly after murders are discovered."

Shaw said, "I don't believe in coincidences."

"Don't you? I would think that would make life quite difficult. Never mind. You wanted to ask me questions, didn't you? Instead of arguing over semantics and quibbling over belief systems."

Shaw looked at Myrtle's hand, where she still held a notebook. "I see you're taking notes."

"I see that you are."

Shaw suddenly looked weary, as if he weren't really up to doing verbal battle with an octogenarian. "Yes, well, it's my job."

"It's mine, too. I'm reporting for the *Bradley Bugle* this evening. You can ask Red for confirmation."

Shaw's brows knit together. "I thought Red told me he hates that you're a reporter."

"He hates when I'm a *crime* reporter. But Red absolutely adores it when I write puff pieces for the paper. And the reunion was to be the puffiest of puff pieces."

Shaw said, "Until the murder happened."

Myrtle didn't quite like the look Shaw was leveling at her. Surely he couldn't be intimating that she had murdered someone just to have an exciting article in the newspaper. She narrowed her eyes at him.

Shaw continued, "Red mentioned a scavenger hunt. Did the murder happen during the course of that game?"

"It did."

Shaw asked, "Where were you during the game?"

"I was in the gym."

"Can anyone confirm that?" asked Shaw in a grim voice.

"No one else was in the gym with me."

Shaw said, "If you were so bound and determined to report on the reunion, it seems you'd have been walking around with the others."

"Is that a question?"

That tired expression crossed Shaw's features again. "Here's a question. Why didn't you go on the scavenger hunt?"

"Because I didn't feel like it. I knew everyone was going to come back to the gym once the game was over, affording me the opportunity to get photos and a quote from the winner. It seemed like a pointless expenditure of my limited energy to canvas the school looking for places on a list."

Here Myrtle managed to look as frail as her tall, big-boned body could appear. Shaw's expression indicated he didn't quite buy it.

Red called Shaw's name, and he turned and waved a hand to show he would come over. "I'm keeping an eye on you," he said levelly as he walked away. "You're free to leave, for now."

Myrtle watched him go, an ambivalent expression on her face. Was it thrilling to be a murder suspect? Or rather aggravating? She couldn't quite decide.

Regardless of what Shaw said, Myrtle wasn't going anywhere. Her ride was investigating a murder, and she was sure Red hadn't had the presence of mind to call for a backup.

However, she'd underestimated Red's desire to get her away from his crime scene. Minutes later, Miles pulled up in his sedan. He looked at her with concern, clearly not wanting to step out of his car and engage with the remaining former classmates at Myrtle's high school reunion. She sighed and got into his car.

Miles wordlessly started driving, carefully maneuvering around the emergency vehicles that were still arriving on the scene. "So, not the boring reunion you thought you were covering."

"Apparently not."

"Who was the victim this time?" asked Miles.

"The annoying Belinda. The *formerly*-annoying Belinda." Myrtle looked out the window in time to catch Lieutenant Shaw watching her leave through narrowed eyes. "I appear to be a prime suspect."

Miles burst out laughing at this, then stopped when he realized Myrtle was serious. "You're not joking."

"No indeed."

Miles said slowly, "Has Red flipped his wig? Or maybe he thinks you'd be safer locked up in the Bradley jail?"

"Oh, it's not Red. Sadly, Lieutenant Perkins is away on a vacation of some sort. There's a Lieutenant Shaw here, instead. He appears to believe I might be some sort of monster." Myrtle decided perhaps it *was* just a bit thrilling to be considered a killer. 'Murderer' was an unusual moniker for someone in her eighties.

Miles considered this. "If you think about it, you do look rather suspicious to anyone on the outside. You're often at the scene of the crime, discovering the bodies. You're very involved. Your son is the police chief and could be helping to shield you from suspicion or discovery. You could be a serial killer for all Shaw knows. Perhaps he thinks unmasking you will mean a big promotion for him."

"Perhaps. It does make things a bit livelier than usual."

Miles said, "So what happened here? From what you're saying, it sounds as if the killer isn't completely obvious."

"That's correct. The evening started out about as numbingly trite as expected. School colors, old pictures, the works. I took some pictures, got a couple of quotes, and everything was just hunky-dory."

Miles said, "Then I suspect there was a change of pace."

"Correct. Belinda decided a game was in order."

"I'm sure you loved that." Miles hid a smile.

"I decided to opt out. Which ended up being a pity, because now I don't know who the murderer is."

"Because Belinda was slain during the game?" Miles pulled into Myrtle's driveway.

"Correct again. It was a scavenger hunt, which managed to scatter everyone. It was the perfect setup for a murder." Myrtle opened the car door, gesturing for Miles to follow her inside her house.

They settled inside, along with Pasha, Myrtle's feral black cat, who'd been waiting for Myrtle in the shadows by the front door.

Miles was frowning. "It seems as though a scavenger hunt actually *wouldn't* be a good setup for criminal activity, though. Weren't all the participants at the same locations?"

"Ah, that's where you're wrong. The way Belinda devised the game, it was more challenging. Each person had different locations on their cards, or the same locations, but in different orders. She meant it to take at least thirty minutes." Myrtle paused, thinking back to the game. "There was something else interesting. When the participants were about to start playing, Belinda announced that she was planning on catching up with some of them individually." Pasha jumped into Myrtle's lap, and Myrtle scratched Pasha under her chin.

"You're thinking Belinda had something on her mind? That maybe she told a dangerous person something that made them upset?"

Myrtle said, "Precisely. I'm just wondering what that might be. I suppose there's nothing to it but to speak with all my former classmates."

"Won't that be hard to do? Weren't many of them from out of town?"

"All of them but Winston and Frank. But Red asked everyone to stay in Bradley until the investigation was further along. They won't be going anywhere."

Miles raised his eyebrows. "Winston? Is that . . . ?"

"Yes, yes. The same Winston from Greener Pastures Retirement Home. He's very tiresome."

Miles hid a smile. "He seemed to be carrying quite a torch for you."

"Not a torch. Perhaps a match. Winston was just as happy chatting up Gladys."

Miles said, "Sounds like he's an opportunist. Tell me about who attended the reunion."

Myrtle looked at her watch. "Hold on, let me call Sloan first. Maybe there's enough time for him to stick the story in the morning edition."

But when Myrtle called Sloan, she could tell he was incapable of reformatting the newspaper. There was loud country

music playing in the background, people whooping and holler-
ing, and a very startled-sounding Sloan slurring his words.

"Never mind, Sloan. But I need to speak with you tomorrow morning first thing."

"Gotcha, Miz Myrtle."

"First thing!" said Myrtle. She hung up.

"No good?" asked Miles.

"Sloan was completely incapacitated. He must have been
drinking for hours. It's all most annoying." Myrtle sighed. "Anyway, you were asking about the guests at the reunion. I'm going
to refer to the women with the last names I knew them by. Who
knows how many husbands the women have gone through. At
any rate, I don't know what their last names currently are."

"That's fair," said Miles.

"Gladys Pinkerton was one of the ones with me when I
found Belinda's body."

Miles said, "So you found Belinda."

"That's right. Gladys and Winston both accompanied me."

"Were you friends with either of them in high school?"
asked Miles.

"No. Gladys was a groupie for the cheerleaders and Winston
was annoying."

"I didn't realize cheerleaders had groupies," said Miles
thoughtfully.

"Gladys was drawn to bright, shiny objects. I suppose the
cheerleaders qualified."

"Had Gladys seen Belinda recently? Besides at the reunion,
I mean?" asked Miles.

"Allegedly," said Myrtle. "She claims to be Belinda's best friend. They were to go on a cruise later this year."

"You don't think she's telling the truth?"

Myrtle pursed her lips. "The thing is, I could tell in an instant that Belinda was the same old Belinda. She always did care a lot about appearances. Poor Gladys doesn't seem to be exactly made of money. She also appears to require what may be very expensive dental work. She simply doesn't seem to be the kind of companion Belinda would ordinarily choose."

"What kind of companion *would* she choose?"

Myrtle said, "A male companion." She paused, thinking. "Then there was Frank."

"Were you friends with him in high school?"

"Heavens, Miles, how many friends do you think I had? No, we were not friends. He was an athlete. At the reunion, he seemed more interested in showing everyone his high school trophies and reliving his glory days. But who knows? He was genial enough, but certainly had the same opportunity to off Belinda that everyone else did."

Miles asked, "Who else was there? It was a small group?"

"Yes. There was a couple there, the Blackwoods. Both of them had been in our graduating class. Harold is a doctor . . . he's likely retired, I'm guessing." She gave Miles a hard look, as if expecting him to say something negative about a physician working in his mid-eighties.

Miles wisely didn't say a word about Harold's age. "What was he like in school?"

"Studious. He was in my classes, except he was in some sort of accelerated math class. I never could get the hang of algebra.

It seemed like a whole lot of nonsense to me. Evie was dating him even back then. She was studious, as well. I remember the two of them keeping to themselves." Myrtle paused. "As a matter of fact, they were sort of keeping to themselves at the reunion, too. Until Belinda barged in."

"Belinda spoke with them?"

"Well, with Harold," said Myrtle. "Although Evie was trying to horn in. I'll have to find out what they were talking about. It seemed to be something serious, from what I could tell. I don't think Belinda was asking for advice on her rose garden, or something innocuous like that." She remembered how red in the face Harold had been, and how Evie had tried and failed to intervene.

"Sounds like a small number of people at the reunion."

"I'm not quite finished with the attendees. You're making me lose my place, Miles! Let's see. I covered silly Gladys, vain Frank, ridiculous Winston, and the good doctor and his wife. There's Millie Thatcher. I forgot Millie."

Miles said, "Is she forgettable?"

"Actually, she can be. She was always a rather mousy girl in high school, hiding behind cat-eye glasses. She was something of a star student back in the day. But then, she appears to enjoy winning. She won the scavenger hunt."

Miles asked, "What was the prize?"

"Who knows? Belinda took that knowledge to her grave."

"Was Millie friendly with Belinda?" asked Miles.

"Not at the reunion, no. She spent most of her time looking around at all of us with poorly-concealed disdain. Though that might just be her natural expression these days."

Miles asked, "How about back in high school?"

"Oh, heavens no. Belinda would never have hung around with someone like Millie. It would have been antithetical to her entire being."

Miles said, "I'm having a tough time picturing this group as murderous marauders. Do you really think it was an inside job?"

"Of course it was. Belinda was unlikeable. Each one of those people is capable of homicide, believe me. Especially since the weapon was a paint can. What we'll need to do is figure out how best to speak with our suspects."

"A battle plan?" asked Miles.

"Precisely. But I don't have the time to work that out now. I have to work on my front-page story for the paper."

"You said Sloan was incapacitated."

Myrtle said, "Yes, even more than usual. But the story will be printed the *following* morning, of course. Or perhaps Sloan will want to run a special edition."

"Surely that would be expensive."

"Well, it will run on the internet when it comes out, at any rate," said Myrtle. Pasha looked up at her, and Myrtle rubbed her fur as Miles stood to leave. "Thanks for picking me up," said Myrtle, remembering her manners belatedly, as usual.

"My pleasure," said Miles.

"Say, for that battle plan, why don't we go to Bo's Diner tomorrow? We can figure it all out. Besides, I've had a hankering for their biscuits and gravy."

Miles looked a bit green at the idea. His delicate stomach often balked at the grease and excessive butter at the diner. But there was always oatmeal. "Tomorrow's Sunday. Isn't Bo's closed on Sunday?"

"Apparently, Bo doesn't attend church," said Myrtle. "The diner is open."

"What time should I pick you up?"

"Let's say seven. You and I will have been up for hours at that point."

Miles looked as if he thought he might sleep just a bit longer, but acquiesced. As he left, Myrtle was perched at her computer desk, typing away, with Pasha still curled contentedly in the warmth of the chair she'd vacated.

Chapter Five

For some reason, Myrtle simply couldn't get comfortable that night. She thrashed around as if she was at war with the sheets and covers. Then, finally, she surrendered, leaving the bed altogether and opting to work a crossword in her puzzle book. To her surprise, Pasha had elected to stay with Myrtle overnight. The cat had stayed well away from the thrashing Myrtle, though, preferring to keep a wary eye on her from a chair across the room. Now Pasha was bathing herself following a nice meal of chicken and turkey pate.

Myrtle was drinking coffee and keeping an eye on the time. The hands on the clock seemed to be barely moving. It was hard to believe there were hours to go before it was even close to seven o'clock.

At some point, she must have dozed off because she woke with a start to find it was six-thirty. She got ready and waited for Miles, who arrived right on the dot.

Miles looked like she felt. "You didn't sleep, either?" asked Myrtle.

"Not a wink."

"You'll rally," said Myrtle with confidence. "We'll bolster you with coffee."

Miles didn't seem cheered by the prospect. "I'll definitely need a nap later."

"Yes, yes, of course," said Myrtle in that vague tone that indicated she wasn't actually listening very closely.

Minutes later, they were walking into the diner, which had been around and in the same family since Myrtle was a child. Myrtle slid into a high-backed vinyl booth. "It's a pity it's so quiet in here. It could have been a good place to pick up gossip about last night."

"Yes, except the gossip wouldn't have been accurate. After all, you know a lot more about what happened at the high school last night."

"I suppose so," said Myrtle. "It's a good thing it's summer, isn't it? How awful it would be for high school students to go right back to school after such a horrid event."

The door to the outside opened, and Myrtle sat up straighter. "Heavens. That's Harold." She watched as a distinguished-looking man with a full head of white hair and bushy eyebrows came in. He walked with a cane, but stood straight.

"Harold? Suspect Harold?"

"Yes, Harold the doctor. Hold on, I'll wave him down and make him sit with us," said Myrtle.

"Wonderful," said Miles dryly as Myrtle proceeded to make large arm gestures over her head.

Harold, naturally, spotted them immediately and walked over.

"Why don't you join us?" said Myrtle. "We haven't even ordered yet, or gotten our coffees. This is my friend, Miles. He's a former statistician."

"Civil engineer," muttered Miles.

"Physician," said Harold, holding out a hand. Miles shook it.

A waitress quickly came by to ask for their drink orders, then hurried away again.

"The diner hasn't changed much," said Harold thoughtfully as his gaze flitted around the old restaurant.

Myrtle shook her head. "Not at all. Only the staff and ownership has changed."

Harold frowned. "Bo doesn't own the diner?"

"Oh, Bo does. But it's our Bo's grandson."

"I see," said Harold. He looked at the menu. "They didn't have breakfast offerings when we were in high school."

"No, that's been a fairly recent addition. I think it's all very good, though. Don't you, Miles?"

Miles, whose stomach could become upset from even the smell of grease, gave a hesitant nod.

"I'm having biscuits and gravy," said Myrtle. "And perhaps eggs and bacon, too."

Harold gave her a smile. "It's amazing you're able to keep your girlish figure with that sort of breakfast."

"That's very kind of you," said Myrtle.

Miles said, "There's always the oatmeal, if you're looking for something lighter."

"That might be a good option," said Harold.

They chatted for a few minutes about the diner and other changes in Bradley. It turned out Harold, although he didn't live in Bradley, resided in the county and practiced at the hospital there.

The waitress came by with their coffees and waters, took their orders, then bustled off again. Myrtle rather liked this particular waitress. She didn't call them all sweethearts and infantilize Myrtle like some of them did. And she wasn't trying to listen in on their conversation.

Myrtle took the opportunity of a conversational lull to ask, "Harold, isn't Belinda's murder horrid? What do you make of it?"

Harold suddenly looked very sorry that he'd sat with Myrtle. "It's awful. Absolutely awful. I can't believe such a thing happened."

Myrtle said, "It looked as if you were having a very intense conversation with Belinda at the beginning of the scavenger hunt. I can't help but wonder what that was about?"

Harold looked at her with a blank expression. "I didn't have a conversation with Belinda."

Myrtle knitted her brows. "You certainly did. I saw you with my own eyes."

Miles squirmed uneasily in his seat at Myrtle's doggedness.

Harold held Myrtle's gaze, then he shrugged. "If you say so." He spread out his hands. "Unfortunately, I'm struggling with memory issues. Perhaps it would be better if you asked Evie about the conversation you say I had with Belinda."

Myrtle tilted her head to one side. "I see. Some cognitive problems?"

"Apparently. Evie certainly thinks I'm having them. And my primary physician agrees." He shrugged again. "So I can't help you with your question."

Myrtle said, "Let's try another one. How far did you get with your scavenger hunt? And did you see Belinda at any point during the game?"

"Two questions," said Harold, gently rebuking her. "To answer your first, I wasn't feeling particularly motivated to win the game. Not like Millie. She was the big winner, wasn't she?"

Myrtle nodded.

"I visited the restroom during part of the game. Our age, you know. It has its limitations. Then Evie and I just meandered around the school a bit, enjoying the memories."

Myrtle said, "And did you spot Belinda during that time?"

Harold considered this. "I didn't *see* her, no. I did *hear* her, though."

"When was this?"

Harold shook his head. "Time has a way of eluding me these days. It was at some point during the scavenger hunt. They were having an argument."

"Who was?"

"Belinda and Gladys," said Harold. "Although, really, it was Belinda doing the arguing. Gladys was sounding very hurt, but not angry."

"Could you hear what the argument was about?"

Harold drew himself up in his vinyl seat. "Naturally. My mind might be going, but my hearing is completely fine." He pushed back his white hair, revealing a pair of hearing aids. "With the help of technology, that is, which I was using last night. Gladys apparently was under the delusion that she was receiving some sort of inheritance from Belinda."

Myrtle said, "That sounds rather presumptuous of her."

"She said something about their long friendship. But Belinda was very dismissive of that. And quite cold. She stated in no uncertain terms that Gladys wasn't receiving anything in her will. Belinda said something about Gladys living in a fantasy world."

Myrtle asked, "Was there anything else?"

"No. I decided I was eavesdropping and moved along."

The food arrived at the table with the efficient waitress, making sure they had everything they needed. Myrtle looked at the two bowls of oatmeal and was infinitely glad that her breakfast wasn't gloppy. She took a satisfying bite of her biscuit.

"When was the last time you spoke with Belinda before the reunion?" asked Miles.

Harold took a spoonful of oatmeal before replying. "It's been many years. I'm not sure how many. But she and I didn't stay in touch. She might have come back to Bradley for a visit at some point, and maybe I saw her then. After all, Belinda's sister still lives here."

"And you're retired?" asked Miles carefully.

"Oh, yes. Twenty years ago now. I didn't mind seeing patients, but all the changes in technology were annoying to keep up with. I'd just get accustomed to new software when it would suddenly change on me. I figured it was time for me to quit."

Myrtle said, "You and Evie have been married for forever, haven't you?"

"Forever and a day. But not as long as it might have been. I felt I should wait to propose until after I was finished with medical school. It didn't seem fair to saddle Evie with supporting both of us while I was a student."

Myrtle said, "You have children, I suppose?"

"Yes. It's funny to think of them as children. A daughter and a son. One just turned sixty and the other is fifty-seven. But they'll always be my babies, no matter how old they are. And you have Red."

"That's right," said Myrtle. "Not quite as old as your children. I had him rather late."

"Still your baby, though," said Harold.

"I suppose. Sort of a bossy baby, though." Myrtle decided it was far too early in the day to dwell on Red. "And Evie? What did Evie do as a career?"

"She taught elementary school for thirty-five years and has been a wonderful wife and mother. Evie is a sterling person," said Harold.

He paused, as if realizing he hadn't been very solicitous over Myrtle. He looked somberly at her. "I was sorry about Stanley."

Miles looked curiously at Myrtle at the mention of her husband. "Yes, it was all very tragic. Did you know Stanley?"

"No. You know how things were back in school. We didn't hang out with the older kids, did we? They were all far cooler than we were. But I heard good things about him," said Harold.

"Yes, I did, too. Of course, I didn't know him in school, either. I knew who he *was*, considering it was such a small school. But I didn't properly meet him until after I'd returned to Bradley High as a teacher. He was the principal then." Myrtle's tone indicated that was all she had to say about that, and that she'd much prefer to continue speaking about the murder of their former classmate.

Harold didn't get the hint. "Well, I'm very sorry. When I'd heard about the match, I'd thought you both might make the perfect couple. You were both academics. You deserved to head into your golden years together, like Evie and I."

"It sounds as if you make a good team," said Myrtle.

"We are. Of course, it's not all wine and roses, is it? She and I can squabble quite a bit. But it's never over anything important. And we make sure we never go to sleep angry at night. We always make up."

Miles cleared his throat. "What type of medicine do you practice, Harold?"

"General surgery. As I said, though, that's in the past now. You do need a steady hand to operate. A younger hand."

His words made Myrtle glance down at Harold's hand, currently holding a coffee cup. It was anything but steady. In fact, it made Myrtle wonder if Harold might not have a Parkinson's diagnosis in his chart somewhere.

The waitress came over with their bills, and Harold paid them all with a large bill he put on the table. "Please keep the change as appreciation for your excellent service," he said to the waitress politely. She gave a little gasp and something of a curtsy before heading away.

Myrtle and Miles thanked Harold, and he waved their thanks away, dismissively. "I enjoyed catching up and getting to know Miles. And I'm glad to have the chance to see you, Myrtle. Last night, the rest of us were still talking after you left. We decided it might be nice to have a sort of informal memorial service for Belinda. A time of remembrance."

"I think that's an excellent idea," said Myrtle. "Have the details been planned?" She very much didn't want to be left out of this memorial service, as she had for the reunion.

"Not yet. But we all shared our contact information with each other." Harold pulled out his phone, squinting. "If I can remember how to retrieve it."

Myrtle held out her hand. "I'll find it."

It was actually not in his contacts list at all, but in a notes app. Myrtle snapped a photo of the names and phone numbers with her own phone. "Thanks. I suppose that will have to be soon, or else everyone will have left town for their own homes."

"I suppose so," said Harold vaguely. He rubbed his eyes. "That oatmeal is obviously kicking in. I feel as though I might go back to sleep."

"Perhaps you should," said Myrtle. "We all had a long day yesterday."

Harold made his goodbyes and headed out the door.

"What did you make of all that?" asked Miles.

Myrtle frowned. "I'm not entirely sure. It seemed to me that Harold has been curating how he appears in public for some time. It somehow didn't feel completely genuine."

"I thought it all seemed very genuine, actually. He spoke about Evie, admitting it wasn't the perfect relationship. He spoke about putting off getting married because of med school."

Myrtle said, "Yes, but that was all carefully presented too, wasn't it? They always make up before they turn in at night. Harold was so thoughtful not to tie Evie down with marriage until he was out of school and making an income. It seemed so very perfect."

"Maybe it is."

Myrtle scowled. "But relationships aren't. They're messy." Her frown deepened. "As a matter of fact, there's something deep in my memory trying to make its way out."

"How deep?"

"High school deep," said Myrtle. "I want to say there were some shenanigans between Harold and Belinda."

"Well, it wasn't as if Harold and Evie were married back then, after all. And it was high school. Shenanigans are to be expected back then."

Myrtle said, "Perhaps. But this rose to the level of scandal, I want to say. Harold and Evie were practically joined at the hip, even back then. Belinda and Harold ended up with some sort of intense connection, I believe."

"Surely Evie wouldn't want to murder Belinda because of something that occurred back in high school. That was a million years ago."

"Sixty-seven years ago," said Myrtle coldly. "And some people have long memories."

"Although, apparently, not Harold."

"I suppose," said Myrtle. "However, he seemed rather sharp for someone who has dementia."

Miles looked at his watch. "What's on tap for the rest of the day?"

"We haven't gone up to visit Wanda for a while. Perhaps we should drop in."

Miles shifted uncomfortably. "It's rather early to pop in on someone unexpectedly, isn't it?"

"Don't be silly. She'll know we're coming."

Miles said hopefully, "Because we'll call her?"

"Because she's psychic."

Chapter Six

Wanda was their friend and, in a strange twist of fate, a cousin of Miles's. She was a mostly illiterate psychic who lived in a recently spruced-up ramshackle shack covered with hubcaps off the old rural highway. She was also, in many ways, the sharpest person Myrtle knew, and the most generous of friends.

So they left, climbing into Miles's car, and headed off to Wanda's. Sure enough, they were greeted by her in her dusty yard. "Good to see yew," she said.

Myrtle gave her a quick hug. "Good to see you, too."

"Know yew jest had breakfast. But I got yew some waters."

They followed Wanda into the hubcap-covered shack. When her brother, Crazy Dan, had lived with her, it had been a dark, cluttered, horrid space. Miles had always immediately taken out his hand sanitizer when entering Wanda's home. But since Crazy Dan had moved out and—however unlikely—found some woman to marry him, Wanda had turned it into a cozy spot, full of plants and soft blankets. Now there was no hand sanitizer in sight.

They settled onto a threadbare sofa covered with cheerful throws. On a table nearby were the tools of Wanda's trade, in the form of a crystal ball (which Myrtle suspected wasn't really crystal), Tarot cards, and other oddities. Wanda handed them their waters.

"Yew had an adventure last night," noted Wanda.

"Indeed, I did. I'd thought I was going to crash a boring reunion. Instead, I crashed a murder."

Wanda nodded. Her eyes were intense. "Yew were mad yew didn't get invited."

"Naturally. I dislike going to events, but I *deeply* dislike not being invited to them."

Wanda said, "That woman didn't want yew there. Had some unfinished bizness to attend to."

Myrtle leaned forward. "That's very interesting that you say that. Belinda did indeed seem eager to have private conversations with various former classmates."

"She wuz very sick," grated Wanda in her ruined voice. Although Wanda had given up her smoking habit, it still laid claim to her ravaged vocal cords.

"Sick?" inquired Myrtle. "You mean sick in the head?" Which, in Myrtle's mind would explain why Belinda didn't invite Myrtle to the reunion.

"Dyin."

Miles looked at Myrtle. "Did Belinda look sick?"

"Not a bit. She looked, most annoyingly, very good."

Wanda nodded. "Sick down in her guts somewheres."

Myrtle looked thoughtful. "So perhaps Belinda had some things she wanted to get off her chest before her imminent demise. I see. Although I think it's completely absurd to murder someone who's terminally ill."

"They didn't know," croaked Wanda. "At least, most of 'em. One mighta figured it out."

"I'm sure you're right. Belinda wouldn't have wanted to disclose such a thing. She was always one to want to look her best." Myrtle paused. "I suppose that's why Belinda was so eager to hold a reunion at such an odd time, too. It gave her the opportunity to tie up those loose threads she was concerned about. She wouldn't have wanted to wait for the 70th year—she might not have lived to make it."

Wanda leveled a look at Myrtle. "Yer in danger."

"Of course I am. It seems to be a way of life for me. Don't worry. I won't take any unnecessary risks."

Miles said, "You don't happen to have any advice on the suspects, I suppose."

Myrtle and Wanda chorused, "The sight doesn't work that way." Although Wanda's version of the phrase was a bit different.

"Right," said Miles with a sigh.

Wanda said, "Jest remember—things ain't always whut they seem."

"Got it," said Myrtle. "Anything else?"

"Any port in a storm."

Myrtle raised her eyebrows. "I'll keep that in mind." Sensing Wanda was done with her prognostications, she asked, "How is everything else going? How is Crazy Dan?"

"Drivin' his new wife crazy," said Wanda dryly. "I guess, anyway. Hadn't heard from 'em."

Miles cleared his throat. "What's the name of Dan's wife?" He preferred to avoid using the "crazy" moniker.

"Tammy Jo."

Myrtle said briskly, "Well, good for Tammy Jo for nabbing Crazy Dan's heart and whisking him away from here. The house has never looked better."

Wanda gave her a gap-toothed smile. "Thanks. Yeah, Dan wuz a mess."

Miles looked thoughtful. "I saw someone I could have sworn was Dan in town the other day. But in a car with a woman I didn't recognize."

"Probly him an' Tammy Jo. Still come to town from time to time. Whud th' car look like?"

Miles said, "I seem to remember a Pontiac Firebird with a rusted hood and fuzzy dice hanging from the rearview mirror."

"What startling recall you have, Miles," said Myrtle.

"That wuz them," confirmed Wanda. "Tammy Jo loves that car."

"Remind me where the two love birds met," said Myrtle.

"County fair. She wuz runnin' the ring toss booth."

"That's very sweet," said Myrtle. "But enough of Tammy Jo and your brother. Tell me about your patron. Lady-what's-her-name."

Wanda had a wealthy English patron who had sort of sub-contracted her out for readings and advice. The income she was making from the woman was moving her steadily toward the middle class. She also made money from the local newspaper for writing amazingly specific horoscopes, which had made her a Bradley phenomenon.

"Lady Cassandra Hawthorne. I guess now she thinks we're friends, 'cause she asked me to call her Cassie." Wanda grimaced. "Don't sit right with me to be that familiar."

"Still, that's very nice. What sorts of advice is she asking about?" Myrtle was quite interested. Apparently, the very wealthy and titled had the same struggles as retired schoolteachers. Or, at least, it was pleasant to think so.

Miles said, "I would think that would fall under client confidentiality."

"Don't be so prudish, Miles! It's not as if Wanda is a doctor, therapist, or priest. Her conversations are more similar to beautician and client." But Myrtle turned to Wanda to say, "Only if you're comfortable sharing the information, of course. It won't go any further. I'm no gossip."

Wanda shrugged. "Don't think it matters. Ain't like we know ennybody she knows. Wants to talk to a sister she ain't talked to fer years an' years. Now th' sister wants to make up with her. Cassie ain't sure it's a gud idea."

"Hmm. She's right to be wary. The sister might be trying to fleece her for all she's worth," said Miles.

"Mmm-hmm," agreed Wanda. "Then she has these dreams she don't understand. Needs my help workin' through 'em. An' she wanted to know if she should invest in some company. Quantum Quokka or some such." She shrugged again. "That's about it."

Myrtle shook her head. "It's all very interesting, but I don't think I'd want to trade my life for hers." This gave her quite a smug feeling. She stood up, and Miles followed suit.

"Would you like to come back home with us? Miles and I are going to watch Tomorrow's Promise and then come up with a plan of attack for the suspect interviews."

This seemed to come as a surprise to Miles. "Are we?"

"Yes, naturally, Miles. We were supposed to come up with plans at breakfast, but then we had the opportunity to speak with Harold, so those plans were scuttled. And I do think we deserve enough of a break to watch our soap opera. We have at least one taped show that we haven't yet watched."

As usual, Miles flinched at the mention of soap operas.

Wanda was shaking her head. "Can't, but thank yew. Gotta meetin' with Cassie in a bit. I come by when I can."

Chapter Seven

Back in the car, Miles said, "It's fairly amazing that a titled Brit would come across Wanda, isn't it? It's not as if Wanda has a social media presence."

"No. But Wanda's horoscopes are online. And they get quite a bit of views."

"*Locally*, yes," said Miles.

"I suppose it was some freak of serendipity. Or perhaps Lady Hawthorne has people who do things for her."

"Like find backwoods psychics?" asked Miles.

"Why not? I'd think, if you had enough money, you could hire people for practically anything you needed. And Wanda is nothing if not genuine. There isn't a phony bone in her body."

Eventually, they got back to Myrtle's house. Pasha was lounging at the front door. To Myrtle's dismay, she appeared to have brought her a present in the form of a field mouse.

"She hasn't done that in a while," said Myrtle with a sigh. "But sometimes she appears to think I need help perfecting my hunting skills."

Miles looked squeamish. "You'll dispose of it, I presume."

"It's something that has to be handled with great delicacy. We wouldn't want Pasha's feelings hurt."

Miles rolled his eyes. "Of course we wouldn't."

"I think it might be best if you distract Pasha in the house. Then I can get the rake out of the storage shed and toss the poor creature in Erma's yard."

Erma was Myrtle's loathsome next-door neighbor. And, despite Erma's membership in Bradley's garden club and her recent attempts to improve her property, her yard was basically a refuse heap of weeds, thorns, and red clay.

Miles seemed uneasy with his assignment, even though he'd gotten the easier part. "How might I distract Pasha?"

"Food would be the best course of action."

"Kibbles?" asked Miles.

"Heavens, no. Pasha is a carnivore." Myrtle waved at the proof on her front doorstep. "It'll have to be some sort of meat product. I'm out of cat food cans, so find some canned tuna. Or chicken. Or even Spam."

Myrtle unlocked her front door, and Miles called to Pasha in his deep voice. Pasha, perhaps sensing some sort of underhandedness, was loath to follow him.

"Try it again, but pretend you're talking to a baby," said Myrtle impatiently.

Miles cleared his throat and attempted a higher octave. Pasha looked doubtfully at him.

Myrtle strode past Miles and into her house. Pasha quickly followed.

But when Myrtle had stepped back outside to take care of the unfortunate field mouse, she'd found the tiny animal must have been playing dead all along. It had scampered off, likely never to darken Myrtle's doorstep again.

When Myrtle walked inside, she found Miles rummaging through Myrtle's canned goods. He stopped when he saw Myrtle. "Already disposed of?"

"It was still apparently alive. It took its shot at getting away."

Pasha was looking at Myrtle through narrowed eyes, as if wondering why she hadn't entered the house with a mouse dangling from her mouth.

"I'll get Pasha the can. She thought she was doing a great deed, after all, and she deserves a reward," said Myrtle.

"I'd be careful about rewarding that particular behavior. Pasha might get ideas."

But Myrtle was already opening a can of tuna and putting it in a bright pink cat bowl. Pasha now gave her an approving look before gobbling down the food.

After getting Pasha settled, Myrtle poured glasses of sweet tea for herself and Miles, and they sat in the living room to watch *Tomorrow's Promise*.

"Where did we leave off last time?" asked Miles. "We haven't watched for a few days."

"We have lots to catch up on. As I recall, during the last episode, Regina was making mischief again."

Miles frowned. "Who's Regina again?"

"The evil pharmaceutical CEO. She was replacing heart medication with sugar pills at Mercy Hospital to drive down the stock price. Then she can buy it up cheaply. But she didn't realize her estranged mother is a patient there."

Miles nodded. "Okay. That does sound familiar."

"Then there's the hospital intern Destiny. She found out she's not only adopted, she's the offspring of Mercy Hospital's chief of surgery and a Russian princess who's been in a medically-induced coma for the last twenty-five years."

"Right," said Miles. "And this affair between the surgeon and the princess was *before* she was in a coma, correct?"

"Thankfully, yes. But now the surgeon is suffering every day, knowing the princess is in the coma. Last time though, we saw her eyes open."

Miles frowned again. "I'm starting to wonder if I actually saw that episode."

"Oh, I think you'd gone to the restroom. You know how it is with a soap opera. You walk away from the television for a few minutes and a baby is suddenly a teenager."

Myrtle and Miles started watching and drinking their sweet teas. Regina was indeed horrified to find her estranged mother had suffered a terrible health setback due to her own wickedness. The Russian princess appeared to be flickering back to life following her extended coma. It was quite a dramatic scene, in fact. The hospital room was dim, young Destiny was sitting by her birth mother's side, holding her hand, when . . .

Myrtle's doorbell rang. Miles and Myrtle both jumped violently. Even Pasha, usually unflappable, seemed jarred.

"It's like Grand Central Station here sometimes," grouched Myrtle as she stomped to the door.

Standing there, holding flowers and candy, was Frank Lawson. He was grinning broadly at her until he spotted Miles sitting on Myrtle's sofa, looking curiously at him. Frank said hesitantly, "I'm not interrupting anything, am I?"

Myrtle could tell Frank would make an annoyingly persistent suitor. However, she didn't want to scare him off completely—this made the perfect time for her to interview him, after all.

"You're interrupting our soap opera, but it's taped, so it doesn't really matter," said Myrtle, more graciously than she ordinarily would when her show was being disrupted.

Miles, as per usual, flushed with irritation at the disclosure that he was watching a soap opera.

Myrtle took the flowers and candy and ushered Frank in, pointing to a free spot on the sofa. "Frank, this is Miles Bradford. Miles, Frank Lawson and I went to school together once upon a time." Myrtle carefully didn't explain whether Miles was a friend or a suitor. Best to let Frank wonder.

Frank was looking slightly more wilted than he had when he'd first appeared at the door. He was lean and weathered, with thinning white hair. Despite his age, he was still quite muscular, as if he exercised daily. This did not endear him to Myrtle. She was reluctant to exercise, preferring to sit and read. She doubted Frank felt the same.

"It's good to see you again, Myrtle," said Frank, giving Miles a cautious look. Miles, however, was looking rather ambivalent, as if uncertain of what his role was supposed to be in this tableau.

Myrtle wasn't giving Miles any clues, preferring to have him in the background as a way to keep Frank at arm's length. She sat back down. Pasha leaped into her lap, looking judgingly at Frank.

"It's nice to see you, Frank. Of course, you're still local, aren't you? I believe I've spotted you around town from time to time."

Frank nodded. "I'm not in the town limits. I live off the old rural route highway."

This meant Frank was a neighbor of Wanda's.

Myrtle said, "I see. So you probably just come to town every now and then with a list. It's a bit of a drive, isn't it?"

"It is, but I like it out there. It's very peaceful."

It wasn't as if Bradley was much of a bustling town, of course. But out in the sticks, it was certainly even more peaceful.

Frank gave Miles an uneasy look. "How's it going, man?"

Miles smiled politely. "Fine, thanks."

Frank hesitated, seemingly somewhat at a loss for how to approach this potential romantic rival. "I don't remember you growing up? Are you from Bradley?"

Myrtle said, "Oh, Miles is a good deal younger than we are. By about twenty years."

This appeared to flummox Frank. He might not have been positive about what he could offer against a much-younger suitor. "I see," he said unhappily. He tried to figure out more about Miles. "And you grew up here?"

Miles shook his head. "I'm from Atlanta."

"So an urban guy." Frank sounded even more unhappy at the thought that Miles might be a worldly man-about-town.

"I suppose so." Miles politely asked, "What sort of work did you do?"

"Oh, I worked in education. Like Myrtle."

Miles said, "English?"

"I speak it," said Frank, frowning.

"Sorry. I meant, did you teach English?"

Frank's frown deepened. "Physical education. Teaching the next generation healthy habits."

"That's very important," agreed Miles.

Myrtle said, "Miles was a mortgage underwriter."

Miles gritted his teeth. "A civil engineer."

Frank looked even more wilted than he had previously. This was not Myrtle's intended purpose, although she was eager to keep him from courting her. He needed to stick around and not run out the door with his tail between his legs. At least for a while.

Myrtle said, "I'm very glad you came by, Frank."

"Are you?" His face brightened.

"Yes. I wanted to ask you a few questions about what happened last night. I write for the newspaper, you see, and I'm working on a story about poor Belinda."

Frank seemed wary. "I don't know very much about what happened, unfortunately. I'm not sure how much help I could be."

"I'm sure you could be *very* helpful," insisted Myrtle. "You don't mind, do you? It would really be a tremendous favor."

"All right," said Frank, somewhat ungraciously.

Pasha retreated to a straight-backed chair in the corner as Myrtle rose. The cat watched Frank through narrowed eyes.

"Thank you!" said Myrtle cheerily. She pulled out a notebook and a pen from her desk drawer. "Now, let's see. Oh, we'll start out by talking about Belinda. As I recall, you knew her fairly well in high school."

"You must have an excellent memory."

"Well, it was par for the course, wasn't it? You were an athlete and Belinda was a cheerleader. You ran in the same circles," said Myrtle.

Frank brightened a bit more at the reference to his athleticism. Perhaps he thought that was one way he had a leg up on Miles. This was confirmed when he eagerly turned to Miles, asking, "Were you involved in high school sports, too?"

Miles shook his head. "I was on the chess team."

Frank looked stunned. It was unclear whether he was more stunned that schools had chess teams, or at the fact someone would admit to being on one. He turned back to Myrtle.

Myrtle continued, "Did you and Belinda keep in touch after graduating?"

"Well, not so very much. You know how it was back then. Keeping in touch meant writing letters." Frank shrugged, as if written correspondence was something beyond him.

"There *were* telephones," pointed out Myrtle.

"Who had the money to call long-distance?"

"So you didn't keep in touch," said Myrtle in summation.

Frank must have sensed something in Myrtle's tone. "I *did* write letters to other people in our class. Just not Belinda. I do write. In fact, I'm working on a book."

"Reading one or writing one?" asked Myrtle.

"Writing one, of course. On the opioid crisis."

This had the effect of surprising Myrtle a good deal. And surprise hadn't been a feeling she'd been getting from the interview with Frank so far. "Are you? Goodness. That must involve a good deal of research."

Frank's expression shifted somewhat. "Well, it's more of a personal story, you see. More of a memoir, I guess you'd call it. I lost my grandson to drugs."

Myrtle and Miles both made very apologetic sounds at this revelation. "I'm so sorry," said Myrtle. "How awful that must have been."

Frank blinked a few times. "Yeah. Yeah, it hasn't been easy. I actually saw a doctor because of it. One of those head docs, you know."

"A therapist," said Myrtle.

"Yeah. She was the one who told me it might help me to get it down on paper. I mean, who cares if anybody wants to read it or not. At least, that's what I thought when I started writing it. But now, I'm thinking maybe if it got published, it might help other people in my situation. Help them deal with it, you know."

Miles said, "It must have been very difficult for your whole family to process."

Frank looked at him curiously again, as if the sensitive Miles was an entirely different species of human. "It was. It made my relationship with my daughter real hard. I couldn't help but feel like she was partly to blame for my grandson's addiction. Her parenting was lousy, she drank too much, and overall just didn't pay a lot of attention to what he was doing. After Tyler died, I've barely talked to her."

Miles said kindly, "It's good that writing the book is helping."

"Yeah. That and volunteering at the youth center. I talk to the kids there about avoiding drugs and share my family's story. I hope it helps." He made an abrupt change from the painful subject. "Anyway, not sure how we started talking about all that. You were asking about Belinda."

Myrtle said, "Right. So Belinda started the scavenger hunt and everyone left to find the items on the list."

"Except for you," Frank pointed out.

"Indeed. I remained in the gym and waited."

Frank said playfully, "Did anyone *see* you stay in the gym? It seems to me you could have sneaked out later on, killed Belinda, and then gone back to the gym."

Myrtle's voice was cool. "Why would I have done that?"

"Why would anyone? I don't remember you and Belinda being good friends during high school."

"There's no reason we would have been. We didn't run in the same circles. But it wasn't as if I *disliked* Belinda." Myrtle crossed her fingers at the untruth. "The point is that I stayed in the gym. Where did you go during the scavenger hunt?"

"I walked over to the front entrance of the school. I spent time looking at the different trophies in the cases there."

Frank said this in a completely matter-of-fact manner, perhaps unaware of how his interest in his past glories might look to others. It was, as well, completely believable as an alibi. But Myrtle supposed it wouldn't take long for Frank to stop admiring his trophies, hit Belinda over the head with a paint can, then resume his admiration once again.

Miles played into Frank's ego, perhaps to keep him engaged, despite the questioning. Or perhaps Miles was simply interested in Frank's high school experience, quite foreign from his own. "What sports did you play in high school? Football?"

"Football, baseball, wrestling, track."

Miles frowned at this. "I'd have thought some of those sports might have overlapped with one another in terms of practice times and events."

"Oh, they sometimes did, but the coaches always made allowances for me. They were happy enough to have me on their team."

Myrtle said, "Thinking back to Belinda. Do you have any thoughts about who might have done this to her?"

Frank spread out his hands. "Who knows? She was such a sweet girl, you know. Maybe one of the group was just off his rocker and decided to go on a homicidal spree."

"Yes, but a homicidal spree would mean the killer would have wanted to do us all in. There would have been opportunity for multiple murders during the scavenger hunt, but that didn't happen."

Frank shook his head. "Can you imagine if somebody *did* take us all on? I mean, that would have been a real crime scene. A bunch of retirees in a high school. Sounds like a horror film."

Myrtle wanted very much to leave the speculative space and go back to the one where facts mattered. "Belinda was saying before the scavenger hunt that she wanted to speak with various people one-on-one."

"Right. To catch up."

Myrtle asked, "Did Belinda try to catch you alone?"

"Nope. I didn't see her. I guess because the trophy cases weren't on the scavenger hunt. Although they should have been."

Myrtle said, "Did you see Belinda at all with any members of the group?"

"Nope. Oh, wait. Yeah, I saw her with Gladys, I think. Just real briefly. I got the impression Belinda was trying to get away from Gladys, actually."

Myrtle raised her eyebrows. "Did she seem nervous around Gladys? As if she were in danger?"

Frank burst out laughing, much to Myrtle's irritation. "You think Belinda was afraid of Gladys? That little mouse? No way. Belinda was tougher than anybody else at that reunion, myself included. No, I meant that Belinda was trying to get away from Gladys because she was so clingy and annoying."

"Gladys told me she and Belinda were best friends."

Frank laughed again. "You've got to be kidding me. That sounds like Gladys lives in some kind of fantasy world. No, Gladys and Belinda weren't even close in high school. I used to hear Belinda talking about Gladys and laughing about her when she wasn't around. She said Gladys was like some kind of groupie. Just wanted to hang out with the popular kids."

For the first time, Myrtle felt a bit sorry for Gladys. Belinda wasn't the nicest of people and never had been.

Chapter Eight

The doorbell rang, and Myrtle stared at it with consternation. Pasha arched her back, lips drawing back in a hiss at the interruption. Miles resolutely stood up and headed to the door.

Winston Rouse was standing in the door with a box of candy and a handful of flowers. He frowned at Miles, then frowned further when he spotted Frank Lawson inside with Myrtle, his own box of chocolates and flowers lying discarded on the coffee table. Miles made a funny cough that sounded suspiciously like a stifled laugh.

"Maybe this isn't a good time," said Winston slowly.

Myrtle, not wanting to entertain any of her suitors on her own, briskly stated, "It's an excellent time, Winston. Come inside."

"Yes, come on in Winston," said Frank. "I was just leaving."

Winston took this all at face value and came inside. He was wearing a festive red bow tie and sports jacket. His white beard was neatly trimmed, and his eyes twinkled merrily—something that annoyed Myrtle immensely.

Pasha swished her tail a few times as Winston settled on Frank's spot on the sofa. Then Winston rose again, remembering his manners. He extended his hand to Miles. "So good to see you again, my kind sir. Let's see if I can remember your name." He frowned. "Milton?"

"Miles. But it was a good guess," said Miles politely.

"Ah, of course, of course. Miles. But, as I recall, you're quite a reader. So perhaps Milton wasn't too far off-base as a guess. Do you like reading Milton?"

Myrtle wondered with irritation if *anyone* really enjoyed reading Milton. Aside from blowhards who enjoyed bragging about their reading lists.

"*Paradise Lost* is a masterpiece," offered Miles. Myrtle rolled her eyes.

Winston beamed at Miles. "Indeed it is! Indeed it is!"

Winston and Miles carried on like fanboys for a few minutes, talking about the epic poem.

Finally, Myrtle had had enough. "Can we all agree that Homer's epics are better? More accessible? More *entertaining*?"

Reluctantly, Miles and Winston agreed, and the Milton love fest was over.

Winston clearly wasn't completely sure what the situation in Myrtle's house comprised. Was she courting a string of suitors? Was she simply having a lot of visitors? Winston gave Frank's love offerings a wary look before saying, "I'm glad to see you looking so well, my fair maiden."

Myrtle pulled a face at the term. And, perhaps, at being told she looked well. She'd never cared much about her looks, and she certainly would not start in her eighties. "How *should* I look?" she scoffed.

"Well, considering the unfortunate circumstances surrounding the reunion, I'd think you'd look a bit faded. But you're in full bloom!"

Myrtle grunted at this. She wanted to get through this interview as soon as possible since she was feeling as if her ability to handle nonsense was at capacity. "I'm glad you're here, Winston. I'm writing an article for the newspaper about the events of last night. I need to get everyone's perspective on the evening."

Winston bowed formally. "It would be my pleasure."

Miles hid a smile as he saw Myrtle getting increasingly aggravated with the entire situation.

Winston said, "Although, it might behoove me to let you know that the state police seem quite interested in *you*, Myrtle."

"Do they?" Myrtle frowned. That state policeman, the one who *wasn't* Perkins, was quite shortsighted. Shaw, she thought his name was. Although perhaps, if the police were focused on her, she'd find the murderous culprit before they did. That always provided such a pleasant feeling of accomplishment. "What sorts of questions was Shaw asking?"

Winston's eyes twinkled. "He seemed to consider you quite an adventuress. He wanted confirmation you'd stayed in the gymnasium instead of skulking around murdering people."

"And what did you tell him?"

Winson said, "Oh, I told him *no one* could confirm that. I also confirmed you were quite clever and were fully capable of doing anything you set your mind to."

"Lovely." It was a backhanded sort of compliment when someone said you would be excellent at homicide.

"Okay," said Myrtle. "Let's start off with the scavenger hunt."

Winston nodded. "It was a delightful idea, wasn't it? So like Belinda."

"Did you keep up with Belinda after graduating?" asked Miles.

"Oh, goodness yes. I've always found Belinda's company scintillating. And I'm a friend of her sister's."

Myrtle grimaced. Belinda was never scintillating. She forged on. "Since you knew Belinda so well, what did you make of her recently? Did she have anything on her mind? Was she worried about anything?"

"Gracious, yes. She was worried about planning that reunion. Belinda wanted to make it a successful event. You know she could be a perfectionist about that type of thing."

Myrtle said, "What possessed her to have a sixty-seventh reunion?"

"Well, I suppose her health. Yes, certainly. She wouldn't have expected to make it to her seventieth reunion, would she?"

Myrtle raised her eyebrows. This was what Wanda had referred to, although she hadn't thought anyone had known. "Why wouldn't she?"

"Because she had a terminal illness. Some sort of cancer. I'm in contact with Belinda's sister—we were friends in high school and exchange Christmas cards and pleasantries from time to time. I didn't push for information, you understand," said Winston. "I assumed she wouldn't want to talk about it. But she was certainly not long for this earth."

Myrtle and Miles looked at each other. "Was this generally known?" asked Miles. "Did the other attendees at the reunion know this, I mean?"

Winston shook his head. "That, I'm not sure. After all, Belinda might have wanted to keep her health under wraps. I didn't tell anyone, of course. Obviously, I'm disclosing it now, but only because poor Belinda is already gone."

Myrtle said slowly, "I'm mostly trying to figure out why someone would find it necessary to murder Belinda. Considering the fact that she apparently wasn't going to be alive much longer."

"Ah. Yes, that's a conundrum, isn't it?"

Myrtle said, "Back to the scavenger hunt. We took a conversational tangent."

"Yes, yes, my dear, we did. Let's see. I was just saying that Belinda did a nice job with the game. What a fun way for all of us to see the changes in the high school since it was our old stomping ground."

Myrtle asked, "And what were you doing during the scavenger hunt?"

"Playing the game, of course. It would have been fun to win something, you know. Even a blue ribbon. I haven't had a blue ribbon in a long time." Winston had a wistful expression on his face.

"So you were playing the game—going to the different locations on the list."

Winston said slowly, "Well, yes. Of course, I did get distracted at one point. There was a history classroom that had its door open. I'm afraid I might have been lured in by a fascinating replica of a suit of armor. The teacher did an amazing job putting historical facts up on the walls. I might have gotten absorbed." He looked across at Miles to see if his new friend might have found himself similarly absorbed, if put in the same situation.

Miles nodded. "That would have been very interesting."

"Yes. There's not much stimulation at Greener Pastures, you see." Winston shrugged.

Now Myrtle was the one who was going to lead them off on a conversational tangent. "No, there's not. There's only so much intellectual pablum one can take. Why do you put up with it, Winston? I don't understand why you reside at a retirement home."

"Your concern is quite touching, my fair lady," said Winston, beaming at her. "But my decision to live at Greener Pastures was a carefully considered choice. I didn't want to do yard work anymore. I didn't want to cook anymore. And I was spending far too much time on my own. Greener Pastures took care of those problems for me."

Myrtle thought about pushing the point further, then realized she had strayed from her original line of questioning. She sought to find the thread. "Okay. So you got distracted in the history room for a while. Did you see Belinda speaking with anyone? Or hear anything that could give us some clues?"

Winston smiled at her. "Dear Myrtle. So concerned about finding justice for poor Belinda. That's very kind of you."

"Clues, Winston?" she asked, teeth gritted again.

"Let's see. I did notice the good doctor speaking with Belinda."

Myrtle said, "And with Evie."

"No, Evie wasn't actually nearby during this particular conversation. It was just Harold and Belinda."

Myrtle asked, "Did Harold seem a little foggy?"

Winston raised his eyebrows. "Foggy? Cognitively impaired?"

"Yes."

Winston said, "Not a whit. I couldn't overhear the conversation between Harold and Belinda, but from what I could tell, the man was sharp as a tack."

Myrtle gave him an impatient look. "How could you tell that when you couldn't hear the conversation?"

"By his eyes, my fair lady. He was completely focused on Belinda. Hanging on every word." Winston paused. "Sadly, my tenure at Greener Pastures has afforded me the opportunity to see far too many of our compatriots afflicted with dementia. It becomes something one can recognize fairly easily. I didn't spot the telltale signs on Harold's visage."

Before Myrtle could ask more questions, Winston turned to Miles. "You might not realize we're in the presence of a real genius."

"Are we?" asked Miles.

"We certainly are. Myrtle here blew the top off the Mensa exam. The admissions test for those with very high IQs," said Winston, by way of explanation. "She was the smartest person in our high school, bar none. And she always had her hand up in English class. Won every spelling bee and essay contest."

Myrtle shrugged, as if it were all in a day's work. "Parlor tricks."

Winston shook his head. "More than mere parlor tricks. Evidence of real, piercing, intelligence. You could have been anything you wanted to be."

"I was never afflicted with ambition."

Winston continued. "Miles, she even edited the school's literary magazine. Rejected most submissions outright, including one of mine, which she dubbed 'pedestrian.'"

Miles suspected Myrtle was being kind.

Winston asked Miles, "Do you know what she was voted 'most likely to' in the yearbook?"

Miles hadn't remembered seeing that mentioned in the yearbook, but he was willing to hazard a guess. "Most likely to correct the principal's grammar during his speech at graduation?"

Winston chuckled at that. "Well, it *should* have been that. But no. It was 'most likely to rule the world.'"

Miles and Winston looked thoughtfully over at Myrtle.

"Fatal lack of ambition," she reminded them. She steered the conversation back into preferable territory. "Going back to Belinda. Did you notice anything else about her yesterday evening?"

Winston thought for a few moments. "I don't think so. I did notice she parked very poorly outside the school. She managed to end up in two parking spaces at once. I figured she must have been distracted when she drove up." He looked at his watch. "Now, I'm afraid I've taken up far too much of your time. You were probably about to do something important."

Myrtle was relieved to be rid of him. "Probably, yes. And now I should get on with it. I hear there's an unofficial memorial service that's going to be held."

"Indeed. A nice way to meaningfully commemorate the life of a delightful woman." He gave Myrtle and Miles a little bow and took his leave.

Miles said thoughtfully, "You've been very popular today."

"Yes. It's all very surprising. I suspect Frank has no money and wants to combine resources. Winston likely wants someone to do his laundry for him. I have no intention of pursuing either one of them."

The doorbell rang, and Myrtle groaned. "I can't stand it! We'll never finish our show at this rate."

Myrtle was so distracted by her annoyance over the interrupted soap opera that she made the fatal error of not checking to see who was outside on her doorstep. This is how her dreaded neighbor, Erma Sherman, muscled her way into the house.

"Myrtle!" said Erma gleefully. "Two gentleman callers in the same day? At your age! You little minx."

Myrtle, however, was not a little minx. Or a little anything. She put her hands on her hips and looking down at Erma disapprovingly. "They were here to discuss murder."

"With flowers and candy?" Erma gave her braying laugh. "They must have been upset to see Miles here."

"Miles is a friend," said Myrtle scornfully.

"You can tell yourself that as much as you please. But I've never seen a man subject himself to watching soap operas. Now, which one will you choose? I rather fancied the second one, the one with the beard." Erma gave her a leering smile. "Anyway, glad to see you. I wanted to fill you in on the new neighborhood watch we have going on."

Apparently, the very sight of Erma was enough to make Pasha leap into action. Or perhaps it was the fact that Erma was loud. It could also have been the fact that Pasha, like most cats, had an instinct that informed her when someone was allergic to her. She strategically wrapped herself around Erma's legs, carefully rubbing her allergens all over Erma.

Erma shrieked and immediately dissolved into sneezing. "Pasha!" she spat out.

Pasha decided Erma must want even more allergens on her and continued her rubbing activities in earnest. This was enough to make Erma run for the door in surrender.

"I think *that* deserves more tuna," crooned Myrtle. "Darling Pasha."

Pasha smiled a feline smile at Myrtle.

Miles was simply glad Pasha wasn't directing his attentions at him.

"Now," said Myrtle grimly. "No one else had better disturb us. We're watching our show and that's that. Then I'm going to send Sloan the story for tomorrow's paper."

"If you think about it, we've really made good progress today," said Miles as they resumed their spots in front of the television. "We spoke with Harold at the diner. Then Frank and Winston in rapid succession. At this rate, we should have a solution to the murder before the end of the day."

"Hardly," said Myrtle as she pointed the remote at the television. "We still have Millie and Evie to go. And I don't believe they're going to come calling. We'll have to ferret them out."

And they continued watching the show to find that the Russian princess came out of her twenty-five-year coma perfectly unscathed.

Chapter Nine

The rest of the day proceeded as Myrtle had hoped and expected. The soap opera had been outlandish but satisfying. Her article for Sloan had been brilliant and well-received by the editor. Pasha had ended up in a food coma after her second can of tuna and spent the night lurking in the shadows of Myrtle's room again.

The next morning, Myrtle got the paper from her front yard and was pleased to see her story on the front page. Naturally, if it *hadn't* been on the front page, Sloan would have heard from her. She worked the crossword puzzle and, while working it, thought about how best to locate Millie Thatcher and interview her.

Then she recalled it was book club day. This meant that her book club had some rubbishy garbage to discuss. Or, perhaps, rubbishy garbage to ignore while they gossiped with each other, instead. The point of the matter was that Millie Thatcher, stranded in Bradley because of a murder investigation, was in need of something meaningful to do. She'd have no idea that this particular book club had a dearth of any real significance.

It was fortunate Harold had given her everyone's contact information. It was probably the only useful thing he'd provided her with. Then Myrtle checked her emails to see what horrid book they'd been tasked to read for book club this month.

She saw it was one of Blanche's suggestions and grimaced. Blanche was the worst offender. The last time Blanche picked a book, it was *The Sheikh's Unexpected Twins*. The only part that Myrtle had found interesting was when the heroine didn't tell the sheikh about her pregnancy before the camel race.

This month's pick was *Fifty Shades of Earl Grey: A Tea Shop Romance*. Myrtle sighed. How was she to lure an intellectual like Millie to book club under these conditions? She decided obfuscation was in order. Myrtle pulled out her phone and carefully dialed the number Frank had provided for Millie.

A wary, reedy voice soon answered. "Yes? Who's calling?"

"It's Myrtle, dear. Myrtle Clover."

There was a pause on the other end, as if Millie Thatcher couldn't figure out why Myrtle might be phoning her. "Myrtle. Hi. How can I help you?"

"Oh, I thought *I* might help *you*. I understand you and the other out-of-towners aren't allowed to leave Bradley yet."

Millie said slowly, "That's the current state of affairs, yes. Although I'm hoping that restriction will soon be lifted."

"I thought you might be bored to tears by now. That you might be ready for something a bit more intellectually stimulating," said Myrtle. She grimaced a little at her lie. Her book club was many things, but intellectually stimulating it was not.

Now a note of curiosity wove into Millie's voice. "As a matter of fact, I was just ruing the offerings on TV. There isn't much there. Not even on public broadcasting. And if there *is* something, I've already seen it."

"Would you like to come to my book club meeting today? That might be a way for you to pass the time."

Millie demurred. "I wouldn't have read the book."

"Oh, I'm sure you have. It's Dickens. *A Tale of Two Cities*."

Millie suddenly sounded more interested. "One of my all-time favorites."

"Mine, too," said Myrtle. "Such a moving tale of revolution, sacrifice, and redemption. You won't have to say anything if you feel uncomfortable. Just sit back and enjoy the discourse. There are always such fascinating discussions." Myrtle realized she was taking things a bit far, but she didn't know another way to meet up with Millie. Although there was to be a memorial service of sorts for Belinda, Millie was the type of person who might choose not to attend.

Millie said, "The meeting is today?"

"That's right. In a couple of hours. We'll be at Blanche Clark's house. My friend Miles and I will pick you up."

Millie hesitated. "I don't know Blanche, I don't think. Did she go to school with us? Is she our age?"

"A bit younger. Though certainly not young." Blanche was, in fact, decades younger.

Millie asked, "Won't she mind having someone crash her book club?"

"Heavens, no. Blanche will be delighted to have you there." Although, truth be told, Blanche would have been more delighted if Myrtle showed up with an unexpected *male* guest to the book club. But Blanche would definitely be polite.

Myrtle called Miles next. "Looking forward to book club?"

"No, of course not. Was there a reason to?"

Myrtle said, "We're going to include a special guest today. Millie Thatcher."

"Did you get her to come under the guise of it being a *real* book club?"

Myrtle said, "There was no other way to entice her to appear."

"What did you tell her we were reading?" Miles's voice was apprehensive.

"*A Tale of Two Cities.*"

Miles sighed. "I foretell much confusion when book club starts."

"It sounds as if you're as psychic as Wanda is."

Miles said, "It doesn't take a psychic to divine what's coming next."

Miles ended up reluctantly agreeing to pick up both Myrtle and Millie. None of them, of course, had read the actual book that had been picked for the month.

There was the sound of a drill outside Myrtle's front door. "For heaven's sake! What now?" She stomped to the door, cane in hand.

When she opened the door, Red barely spared her a glance. "Hi, Mama."

"Don't you 'hi Mama' me. What in the blue blazes are you doing out here?"

Red eyed the contraption he was installing by her front door. "Keeping you safe."

"What makes you think I need to be kept safe? And that some sort of mechanical device will do it?"

Red finally looked away from the contraption. "Because I know you. And I trust you about as far as I can throw you. You get involved in local murders, which isn't a healthy habit for an octogenarian. Plus, you haven't been wearing your medic alert necklace."

"I'll have you know it's right in my shower. I figured that was the best spot for it, since that's where most home accidents occur."

Red gave her a dour look. "The best spot for it is around your neck."

Myrtle ignored this. She found she ignored many things Red said. It was better than having her temper rise, which couldn't possibly be good for her blood pressure. "What's that thing you're installing?"

"It's a special doorbell. It has a camera on it. We're going to connect it with your phone so you can see who's at the door before you open it."

"So I can avoid people? Like you?" asked Myrtle sweetly.

"So you can avoid murderers," said Red. He straightened, eyeing his handiwork. "There. Now let me see your phone so I can put the app on it."

He followed his mother inside, taking the phone from her and downloading the application. "It'll give you a notification when someone is on your doorstep. You can see the front entrance by going here." He showed her where to go, and Myrtle nodded.

Myrtle could tell he was gearing up for a lecture, which was very tiresome of him. Sure enough, he launched right in. "You know I don't like you doing this investigative journalism nonsense. The thing is, Mama, you push and push and then the next thing you know, somebody comes after you. It happens every time. Just leave it alone. Someone is very dangerous."

"Right."

Red continued, "And that dangerous person *isn't* you. No matter what Shaw thinks."

Myrtle smirked. "He seems to believe I'm a homicidal maniac."

"You're definitely a maniac, but not a homicidal one. It's a pity you feel you've gotta live life on the edge. You should be sitting inside, doing your puzzles, and talking to friends."

Myrtle said, "As a matter of fact, I've done all those things recently. And I'm going to book club with Miles this afternoon."

Red gave her a suspicious look. "Hmm."

Myrtle looked blandly back at him. He wasn't to know she was taking one of his suspects to book club with her.

Red continued. "You can't blame Shaw for thinking you're a good suspect. After all, you're always on the scene of a murder."

"You make it sound as if it's a daily occurrence," said Myrtle with a sniff.

"You're also always looking for something to do."

Myrtle raised her eyebrows. "Are you implying that I'm murdering the good citizens of Bradley just to have a crime to investigate?"

"No. No, I'm not implying that. But I believe it's the direction Shaw's mind is going in. I wouldn't be surprised if he shows up at your door soon to speak with you again."

Myrtle said, "Than I shall simply screen my visitors with my handy new doorbell app."

Red said, "I haven't even asked how the reunion was."

"You mean before the murder?" Myrtle shrugged. "It reminded me why I disliked high school. The nice thing was that I was reporting on it, so I could view the entire event through a lens."

"You weren't close with any of those folks?"

"Absolutely not," said Myrtle icily. "And it rather offends me that you think I could have been."

"Who *did* you hang out with? Anybody stand out?"

Myrtle pursed her lips. "I was in the journalism room quite a bit. I had a few good friends—earnest, academic, enthusiastic readers. They're all dead now."

Red looked as if he was sorry that he asked. He cleared his throat. "Well, that stinks."

"It's par for the course when you're very old."

Red looked at his watch. "I should be heading out of here. It would be a good idea if you wore your medic alert necklace *and* used the doorbell."

Myrtle waved him off. "I'm perfectly safe in my ivory tower, especially after your front door embellishments. Besides, people come and go here with alarming frequency. I don't think a murderer would dare darken my doorstep."

Red hurried off, presumably to work on the investigation, and Myrtle experimented with her doorbell app for a few minutes. It was remarkably easy to use. She figured it would be an excellent tool in her avoidance of Erma Sherman.

Chapter Ten

Later, Miles picked her up for book club. "Do we know where this Millie is?"

"At the only hotel in the area. I'm sure she'll be waiting outside for us. She's the sort of person who's always on time."

Sure enough, Millie was waiting outside the hotel when Miles pulled up. She was wearing the same dress she'd had on for the reunion. It occurred to Myrtle that no one had prepared to spend more than a night in Bradley.

Millie said as much when she climbed into the car. "I didn't bring many clothes for the reunion."

"Of course you didn't. No one would have expected a murder to take place at the high school. Millie, this is my friend Miles."

Miles greeted her politely, then started driving toward Blanche's house.

Millie was still fretting over showing up uninvited at book club. "I spent a little time online reviewing the book."

"Did you, dear?" asked Myrtle vaguely.

"Yes. It's been a while since I've read *A Tale of Two Cities*. I wanted to make sure I could contribute intelligently to the conversation."

Miles gave Myrtle a sideways look. Myrtle said, "I've no doubt you'll have the most thoughtful ideas on the novel." Especially since Millie would be, unknowingly, offering comments on that trashy book Blanche had picked out.

Despite being right on time, the book club meeting was in full swing when they arrived. That was likely because Blanche enjoyed throwing parties. As far as Myrtle could tell, she cared nothing for reading or books in general. But she enjoyed having people over and entertaining, often with a signature drink and plenty of other alcohol options.

Blanche's house was something of a showplace. She tired of her décor every couple of years and would completely redecorate. The current iteration was very heavy on antiques. The formal living room had pale blue silk wallpaper, French antiques, and crystal sconces casting warm light. The sofas were cream-colored sentinels and seemed to judge anyone crass enough to sit on them.

Millie trailed in behind them, looking overwhelmed. Blanche spotted them and immediately came over, thrusting drinks in their hands from a nearby table. She was wearing flowing palazzo pants in a dramatic black and white geometric print. "Try my signature cocktail for today's meeting," she demanded.

Myrtle could tell Blanche had already enjoyed quite a bit of her signature cocktail. Myrtle said, "You know I'm not much of a tippler, Blanche. I'll abstain today."

Miles was looking around for a quiet corner and was immediately targeted by Blanche. "Miles, you'll do it, won't you? I've worked so hard on these drinks."

Myrtle would have called this peer pressure, but Miles and Blanche were not contemporaries.

Miles was also too polite. And he might already tell that Millie was going to spurn the drink like Myrtle had. "Thank you," he said.

He took a cautious sip while Blanche watched with bated breath. Then Miles coughed. "It's wonderful, really."

"Isn't it?" beamed Blanche. "That makes me so happy that you like it, too. And who do we have here, Myrtle? A PNM?"

"PNM?" asked Myrtle.

"That's sorority speak. It means 'prospective new member.'"

Myrtle didn't think Blanche had been in a sorority for quite a long time. She said, "This is Millie Thatcher. Millie, this is Blanche. Millie was a classmate of mine and is back in town for a visit."

Blanche's kohl-rimmed eyes widened dramatically. "You were at that ill-fated reunion?"

Millie shifted uncomfortably on her feet at her association with a murderous local event. "Yes."

"I was there, too," said Myrtle in a vexed voice.

Blanche said, "Were you? That was your reunion?"

"I just said that Millie and I were classmates." Myrtle's eyebrows lowered.

Blanche waved a manicured hand. "Of course, of course! Well, proceed. I want to hear all about it."

At that point, though, a couple of other book club members pulled Blanche away into another conversation.

"This is a very lively book club," said Millie slowly as two members whooped and hollered behind them.

"Is it? I suppose it is," said Myrtle. "They do love Dickens." She needed Millie to stay until the bitter end, so decided she wouldn't disclose the true nature of the club. Instead, she turned to Miles and asked, "How was that drink? Was it as noxious as it appeared?"

Miles was still holding the cocktail, albeit at a safe distance. "It was. Is there an appropriate houseplant to dump the liquid in? Blanche added far too much lavender syrup. It tasted like bad medicine." He looked nervously toward Blanche, as if concerned she was going to come galloping back over and ply him with the foul-tasting beverage again.

"No one else seems to notice," said Millie, frowning. And indeed, the other book club members were happily imbibing.

Myrtle was worried that someone would come over and interrupt their conversation. Most likely the horrid Erma Sherman, who was always nosy about new faces. She decided she needed to find out what Millie knew about Belinda's death while she could.

"Listen, Millie," said Myrtle. "What did you make of that reunion?"

Millie made a face. Apparently, she was happy to make disparaging statements about Belinda's event, regardless of Belinda's untimely death at the end. "It was pretty horrid, wasn't it? In that dreary gym? With a silly game to play?"

Myrtle lifted an eyebrow. "As I recall, you *won* the silly game."

Millie shrugged a thin shoulder. "I play to win, even if the game is ridiculous."

"Have you kept in touch with Belinda over the years?"

Millie scowled at her. "Of course not. I couldn't stand the woman. I didn't murder her, but I applaud the person who did. Belinda was a waste of space."

"Obviously, you were not friendly in high school," said Myrtle.

"No. Belinda was constantly pestering me to let her copy my homework or cheat off my tests. She was the most entitled person I think I've ever met. She didn't seem to think that she should have to study or do schoolwork at all. But she still wanted excellent grades, without the work."

It sounded about right. Myrtle had no problem imagining Belinda as one of those types of students.

Millie asked her, "Did you spend much time with Belinda in high school?"

"Absolutely not. I did my best to avoid her. Quite successfully, I might add."

"Lucky you," said Millie sourly.

"What were you doing during the scavenger hunt?"

"Winning it," said Millie. "Why? Did you think I still had time to kill Belinda during the game?"

"Don't be silly. I was merely curious whether you saw or heard anything. As distasteful as it might be, *someone* in our group murdered Belinda."

Millie sighed. "I've already talked about this with you before."

Myrtle frowned, a sudden memory trying to surface. "I seem to remember something from long ago." It was because of Millie talking about her desire to win and because she'd mentioned Belinda's equal desire to cheat.

Millie gave her an uncomfortable look, as if she could see where this might be going.

Miles observed Myrtle's memory at work. It was always excellent, even when the recollection she was dredging up was from over sixty years ago. "Wasn't there something that happened between the two of you? Back in high school?"

Millie gave her a disdainful look. "I don't know what you're talking about."

"Surely you must. You were talking about it quite a bit back then. Something Belinda stole from you."

Millie colored. "You must be misremembering. It's only natural at our age."

"My mind is clear as a bell," said Myrtle. "And it's all coming back to me. Belinda claimed a research project or some such as hers. But you said you'd done all the work."

Millie's voice was flat. "You're mistaken, Myrtle."

Myrtle realized she wouldn't get much further with Millie on that particular subject. "Tell me what you've been doing recently. Are you still working?"

Millie nodded. "Just some part-time work at the community college."

Miles was getting very good at not expressing outward surprise at octogenarians in the workforce.

Millie said, "How about you, Myrtle? Still teaching?"

"Gracious, no. I gave that up long ago. Now I've been retired longer than I ever taught. But I do work for the newspaper from time to time. I have a column with them, and I also do crime reporting."

Millie's eyebrows shot up again. "I see. So you're writing a story on Belinda's death. I knew you were writing up the reunion, of course."

"Yes. That reunion piece has gotten superseded by the murder."

Millie said, "This conversation is off-the-record."

"Yes. I just gather information and see what I can do with the odds and ends." Myrtle made it sound as innocuous as possible.

Millie looked sternly at Myrtle. "As long as we're on the same page." She paused, then said, "I'm sure Gladys might be at fault."

"Everyone seems to think that," said Myrtle.

Millie's stern look deepened. She apparently didn't like being one of the crowd, especially *that* crowd. "Well, it's an easy conclusion to come to. From what I hear from the others, Gladys didn't really live in reality. She seemed to think she and Belinda were very close. But Belinda didn't feel the same."

Myrtle said, "So, I'm trying to put together this scenario in my head. If Gladys murdered Belinda, this means that Belinda must have shattered this illusion that Gladys had about their friendship. Is that what you're saying?"

"Right. Gladys thought Belinda and she were besties. Then Belinda probably got sick of having Gladys be so annoying, and told her off. Maybe she told her off in front of others and Gladys felt humiliated. Gladys stormed after Belinda and hit her with the can of paint."

Myrtle raised her eyebrows. "You weren't with our little group who discovered Belinda. How do you know about the paint can?"

"Please. Do you really think the others weren't going to talk about the murder weapon. You're overestimating them, if you do."

Millie's tone was getting under Myrtle's skin. Miles, being a good sidekick, stepped in to give Myrtle time to regain her patience. He cleared his throat. "Did you see anything or hear anything during the scavenger hunt that might be helpful? It sounds as if you might have been all over the school, for the game. It seems you might have seen or heard things."

Millie straightened up a bit. Myrtle thought appealing to Millie's ego wasn't a bad idea. Millie said, "That's true. I did see Harold sneaking a quick cigarette outside the school. I was rather shocked by that. A surgeon, smoking? He told me not to tell Evie."

Further questioning was interrupted by Blanche, who'd torn herself away from her various conversations to start the book club meeting.

Chapter Eleven

"**A**ll right, everyone," said Blanche merrily. "Let's take our seats and discuss this marvelous book. At least, *I* really enjoyed it. Why don't we give it a round of applause?"

There was rather tepid applause for *Fifty Shades of Earl Grey: A Tea Shop Romance*. Millie was applauding enthusiastically, thinking it was for *A Tale of Two Cities*. Myrtle and Miles followed suit, which made the other book club members stare at them in surprise.

Blanche beamed at the three of them, then waved a hand at Millie. "Let's all be sure to welcome our guest today. If you haven't yet met her, the delightful Millie Thatcher is here with Myrtle and Miles."

The applause now was stronger, the ladies wanting to be polite to a guest. Georgia Simpson, a large, tough woman with big hair that never moved, and rife with tattoos, whooped loudly in welcome.

Millie seemed quite stunned by the response. She nodded shyly, coloring a little.

Then Blanche seemed to lose track of what she should have been doing. Myrtle muttered to Miles, "Too much of that lavender signature cocktail."

Indeed, Blanche started rambling about things that had nothing to do with books whatsoever. Fortunately, Tippy Chambers, the presiding president of book club as well as many other local clubs and organizations, stepped in. Her small dog, Weesa, peeked out of her purse, glaring at the assembled club members. Myrtle didn't recall seeing Weesa at book club before, at least not at other members' houses. Perhaps it was a lapse on Tippy's part. Or perhaps Blanche had issued a special invitation to Weesa.

Regardless, Tippy quickly got them back on track. "Thank you, Blanche. Let's go ahead now and talk a little about this month's selection, a pick by our hostess."

Blanche gave an exaggerated bow, resulting in a sloppy spill from her glass to the front of her designer top.

Erma was loudly telling some poor soul that she couldn't drink the lavender drink because it was sure to disturb her digestion. Then she started a monologue about her other digestive issues until Weesa gave a sharp bark from Tippy's purse. Erma quickly stopped talking.

Tippy continued, "Who'd like to talk about their impressions first?"

Millie raised her hand. This gave Myrtle a sudden flashback to her high school days. She recalled that Millie always seemed to have her hand up in the air, no matter what the subject was.

"Millie?" Tippy beamed at her. "How generous of our guest to have read the book!" Tippy didn't say that it was more than many of the regulars probably had done, but the inference was there.

Millie was emboldened by the friendly nature of the assembled club members. She moistened her lips, then stood up. "I'll start by saying that it wasn't a hardship to read this book at all, considering it's one of my favorites."

There was a surprised murmur in the crowd. Blanche said, "Fancy that!"

"I think the part that resonates with me most is the theme of sacrifice."

Tippy thought this through, nodding. "True. The poor heroine had to choose between her small tea shop and Earl's corporate empire."

Millie gave Tippy a sideways look, possibly wondering if she'd imbibed too many of Blanche's cocktails. She continued talking about *A Tale of Two Cities*, "Class differences are also a theme, of course, the importance of which can't be discounted."

"That's right!" said Blanche from her perch on the arm of one of her expensive sofas. "The tea dynasty."

Millie frowned, as if trying to remember mention of a tea dynasty in Dickens' masterpiece. "Okay," she said slowly. She paused, as if struggling to pick up where she left off. "Then we have the imprisonment."

Tippy nodded.

Blanche, though, looked thoroughly confused. "Imprisonment? I must have missed that chapter. I skim sometimes when there's too much description."

Tippy said, "I believe Millie is talking about metaphorical imprisonment. The corporate tea contracts in the story."

Erma gave a melodramatic sigh, clutching the area where her heart should be. "When Earl gives up his corporate takeover to save her little shop? It made me tear up!"

Millie now seemed even more confused than Blanche. "No, I was speaking of literal imprisonment, not metaphorical imprisonment. In the Bastille."

Miles grabbed Myrtle's sleeve, giving her a panicked look. "Our pretense is totally falling apart. Right in front of us."

She shook him off. "Don't worry, Miles. This is the fun part. Look how confused everyone is. Besides, we finished interviewing Millie."

But Miles seemed so embarrassed on either Millie's behalf or Tippy and Blanche's that he took out his hand sanitizer as if he could rid himself of his discomfort that way.

Myrtle took pity on him and spoke up. "Thank you, Millie, for your astute observations. Now perhaps we should let someone else give their impressions."

Millie nodded slowly. "Sure. Maybe that's a good idea. I mean, it's been a little while since I read the book, after all. Even if it is a favorite of mine. Maybe you could share some thoughts on the story."

"Certainly," said Myrtle briskly. Naturally, she hadn't read the ridiculous excuse of a book club book. But she'd taught *A Tale of Two Cities* mercilessly for years. She could certainly relieve Miles of his discomfort and make Millie feel better, too. "Of course, what really interested me was all the business about the French."

Georgia bellowed, "French? Don't remember any French in the book. Unless you count that fancy Earl Grey learning about tea in Paris."

"There was that," agreed Erma, nodding sagely.

Tippy said, "Earl Grey wasn't actually French."

Myrtle reflected that Tippy could sound condescending sometimes, despite her best efforts.

Sherry, Myrtle's neighbor, had apparently enjoyed the signature cocktails a wee bit too much. She slurred, "My ex-brother-in-law married a French woman."

The conversation suddenly lurched over to France. Erma, never one who liked to be left out, said, "I've had a couple of French maladies! The doctors said so. *Mal de tête* and *Mal de ventre*."

Myrtle rolled her eyes at Miles. "Headache and stomachache."

Everyone began talking at once now, and in small groups. Myrtle shook her head. "We should go. Book club is effectively over."

Millie knit her brows. "We haven't really fleshed out the book. There's so much left to uncover."

"How about if the three of us have an intelligent conversation about *A Tale of Two Cities* in the car on the way to your hotel? I can promise you that the rest of this book club meeting is dissolving into madness. All the signs are there."

Millie frowned, looking at the surrounding group. Erma was now making a special announcement about the importance of their neighborhood watch program. Millie slowly nodded.

They climbed into Miles's car, and Myrtle gave a sigh of relief at escaping. "There. That's done."

Millie said, "This is a non-sequitur, but something else happened at the reunion. I mean, since you're getting background for your article. It was Frank Lawson. I overheard him talking with Belinda in one classroom when I was heading for the cafeteria during the game. He was angry with her."

This seemed to be a common theme for everyone at the reunion.

Millie continued, "It was about his grandson."

"Ah. Yes, Frank told Miles and me about his tragic death. A drug overdose, I understand. Horrid."

Millie nodded as Miles started slowly driving away from Blanche's house. "Yes. But the thing is, he seemed to be blaming Belinda for his death."

"*Belinda*? You can't tell me she was a drug dealer. Not at her age. Surely that's one occupation unsuited for an octogenarian."

Millie said, "I didn't hear all of the conversation, of course. But it sounded like Belinda was directly involved. Something about a clinic? Some kind of connection to a clinic?"

Miles said, "So it sounded as if Frank blamed Belinda somehow?"

"Exactly," said Millie.

The rest of the time, the three engaged in an intelligent and spirited discussion of *A Tale of Two Cities*, much to Millie's delight and enjoyment.

After dropping Millie off, Miles said, "I guess we're heading back to your place?"

"Let's. Dusty was supposed to come today to tackle the yard. It was starting to look like a jungle out there. I'd like to make sure he's actually there."

Dusty was Myrtle's ancient yardman. He was not fond of his occupation and looked for opportunities to get out of yard maintenance tasks as often as possible. His laziness, however, was surpassed by his wife, Puddin. Puddin was Myrtle's housekeeper and very difficult to lure to the house.

Myrtle, then, was pleasantly surprised to see Dusty working in the yard. Puddin was sitting on Myrtle's front porch as if she hadn't a care in the world.

"I have to say, I'm amazed," said Miles. "How were you able to get those two to come over?"

"Well, I really lit into Dusty. Said I was going to have to wrangle the overgrowth, myself. Dusty doesn't seem to want me to hurt myself, so I'll occasionally try that particular threat. It often works, but not this quickly."

Miles said, "If he's not working, then he's not making money, of course. Seems as if he might have been interested in income."

"True. I guess Puddin is along for the ride, but I'm going to make her come in. The kitchen could use wiping down, among other things."

Puddin's expression darkened when she spotted Miles and Myrtle pulling into the driveway. She looked rapidly from her left to her right, as if searching for an escape avenue.

"Not getting away this time," said Myrtle grimly.

Puddin seemed to come to the same conclusion. She ended up slumping on the front porch in resignation.

"You're a sight for sore eyes," said Myrtle as she stepped out of the vehicle.

Puddin's pale face held a sour expression. "Why're your eyes sore?"

"It's an expression," said Myrtle in irritation.

Miles said, "Myrtle, I'm heading home." He'd apparently had enough of socializing following the book club meeting. He swiftly drove away.

Puddin said, "I just cleaned for you, you know."

"Just? I guess 'just' is relative. It's been over a month."

Puddin muttered, "Seems like just yesterday."

"My kitchen is a disgrace. It needs to be wiped down, especially the fridge and the stovetop."

"My back is thrown," said Puddin.

"You know I don't even listen to that excuse anymore. In fact, I've come to the conclusion that your back is hale and hearty. And, of course, a lot younger than mine. Come on inside."

Puddin shambled behind Myrtle as slowly as possible. She put her hands on her hips. "Looks clean to me."

"If this looks clean to you, your home must be in a terrible state of affairs."

Puddin squinted at her. "It's clean, if that's what you're sayin'." She followed Myrtle into the kitchen, where Myrtle pointed out the wretched state of the appliances and some other shortcomings of the room. Puddin, with resignation, pulled out cleaning supplies from underneath Myrtle's sink.

"Those are mine," said Myrtle.

"Didn't bring mine, did I?" said Puddin pointedly. Eager to change the subject from cleaning, she said, "Heard about that murder at the high school?"

"I was there. I wrote an article about it."

Puddin ignored this, instead filling Myrtle in with mostly inaccurate information about the deadly event, scraped together via various gossips in Bradley. "Reckon she had it comin' to her," said Puddin, viciously scrubbing at Myrtle's coffee pot.

"Why would you say that?"

Puddin shot her a look, as if questioning Myrtle's cognitive ability. "Because she's done been murdered."

"That doesn't mean she deserved it. Plenty of people get murdered every day because they were just in the wrong place at the wrong time."

Puddin snorted derisively. "That's what you think. An' look at that woman. Bet she got on somebody's bad side."

Myrtle thought Belinda had actually gotten on *many* people's bad side.

Puddin said, "I went to high school there, you know."

Myrtle frowned. "You didn't come through my classroom. I don't remember your being there at all."

Puddin shrugged. "I didn't come to school a lot."

"Why on earth not? You'd have ensured a better future for yourself."

"Naw. I didn't want to be a bigwig. Not like you." It sounded like quite an accusation coming from Puddin.

"No one in this town would consider me any sort of bigwig. I'm a retired English teacher. I make a pittance. A pittance!"

There was a knock on the kitchen door, which lead to the backyard. Dusty stood there, looking laconically at Myrtle. "Took care of them weeds."

"What weeds?" asked Myrtle suspiciously.

"The ones you told me to get rid of."

"I did no such thing," said Myrtle. "You must be confusing me with someone else. I don't have any weeds in my yard."

Dusty scowled. "They're done pulled up."

"Let me see these so-called weeds."

Which was when Myrtle followed Dusty to the back yard and discovered that he had pulled up some new perennials and the herbs Wanda had given her for a small garden.

"Those are legitimate plants, Dusty!"

Dusty spat on the ground very near the eviscerated vegetation. "Look like weeds."

Myrtle counted to ten. It was one of many times she wished she could fire this husband-and-wife pair. But, as previously mentioned, her pittance of retirement pay wouldn't allow her to upgrade to a better team. Plus, she knew if she told Dusty to leave and not come back, he'd happily take her at her word. Still, there should be repercussions to this lackadaisical attitude toward her yard and its flora.

"Dusty, this is not good. These were plants that were important to me."

Puddin peered at the sad pile on the ground and sniffed. "Look like weeds."

"Like I said," said Dusty.

Puddin shifted her focus to Myrtle's face. "Yer gettin' red. Not havin' a heart attack, right?" She crossed herself, despite being Baptist.

"No, I'm just fine. But there should be reparations paid."

Puddin frowned again. "Speak English."

"Dusty should pay for what he did."

Dusty howled like a basset hound. "We ain't got no money!"

"Nope!" said Puddin. "Not a red cent."

"I don't want your money. But I think, under the circumstances, the least you can do is to pull out my gnomes for me. Without renumeration."

"Englishhhh," hissed Puddin.

"Without being paid. I'll pay you for cutting the grass, of course. And for Puddin's sorry excuse for cleaning."

"Hey!" said Puddin.

Dusty sighed. "Okay. I'll pull 'em out. What's Red done this time?"

"What *hasn't* Red done? He changed my thermostat settings without telling me, for one. It was freezing cold in my house when he left."

Dusty and Puddin looked doubtfully at each other. "It's purty hot in yer house," said Puddin.

"Then he hired somebody to clean my gutters. They're *my* gutters, and I have my own person to do them."

Dusty said, "I dunno Sounds like a good son to me."

"Then he installed a doorbell with a camera on it. That was really the last straw. Red simply cannot mind his own business."

Which was when her phone suddenly chirped at her to let her know someone was at her door. They all looked at her phone.

Myrtle swiped at the device a few times. Then she frowned down at it. "Erma Sherman is at my door."

"Well now," said Dusty. "Sounds like you oughta be glad about that doorbell Red done got you."

This annoyed Myrtle even more. "Still, I'd like those gnomes out, posthaste. Thank you, Dusty." With this, she went inside her house, where she hid until Erma went away.

Chapter Twelve

Myrtle knew she should be worn out after the events of the day. The book club had been trying, as had wrangling Puddin and Dusty. However, she felt energized. She thought about phoning Miles to see if he wanted to interview Evie Blackwood. Harold's wife was the last suspect, and Myrtle would like to cross her off the list. Despite the nonsense that had tried to hijack the day, she felt as if she and Miles had made progress. However, Miles had looked tired and ready to escape when he'd left her house earlier. If she called him, he'd likely be cross, and she wasn't in the mood to deal with a sullen Miles.

She decided she was perfectly capable of speaking with Evie herself. The only problem was that the hotel wasn't particularly close to Myrtle's house. Although she certainly did feel energetic, that feeling wouldn't last after a long July walk.

So she picked up the phone, calling Evie with the helpful phone list Harold had provided. Evie picked up, sounding slightly suspicious, as if she suspected the unknown number might end up being spam.

"Evie? It's Myrtle Clover. How are you today, dear?"

Evie, although no longer suspicious, didn't sound exactly pleased to hear Myrtle's voice on the other end of the line. "I suppose I'm as well as I *can* be, under the circumstances. Of course, it's challenging being here in the hotel."

"I'm a little surprised you and Harold are in the hotel at all. It sounds like your house isn't too far away."

Evie said, "We asked that policeman, and he told us he wanted everyone in town, at least for right now. Not slightly outside of town."

"How dreary, staying in a hotel. That's actually the reason I was calling you. I thought you might want to come over to my house for a little while. We could visit and catch up. You're still driving?"

Driving, of course, was key.

"I'm driving, yes. Of course, Harold could drive me over, too."

This didn't suit Myrtle, however. She'd already spoken to Harold. Plus, she thought she could get more information from Evie without Harold nearby. "I thought it could be just girls this time," said Myrtle, trying to sound sweet.

Evie hesitated before saying, "All right, Myrtle. That sounds good. When should I come over? And where do you live?"

Myrtle quickly gave her the address and added, "Come by right now. I'm not doing a thing."

A few minutes later, Myrtle's doorbell app showed Evie driving into the driveway and then walking up to the door. Myrtle greeted Evie with a show of affection she'd never have been able to pull off in high school. Evie looked rather stunned by Myrtle's effusive display. "Uh, hi," she said.

"Come in, come in!" said Myrtle merrily. "It's so very good to see you. Heavens, it's been a long time."

"Technically, it was just a couple of days ago," said Evie.

"Yes, but I was working. I'm a journalist, of course, so I wasn't able to socialize as well as I'd have liked. This is much better."

Evie looked as if she wasn't entirely sure that was true.

"I have some cookies and milk," offered Myrtle. They were the offerings she kept on hand for when her preschool grandson came over, but would work just as well for Evie.

They headed into the kitchen where Myrtle had set up a plate of store-bought chocolate chip cookies and a small pitcher of milk. "There now," she said. "Isn't this nice?"

Evie gave her a weak smile.

"I'm thinking this type of get-together, something small and intimate, would have worked better than Belinda's larger-scale reunion," said Myrtle.

Evie nodded. "You're right. We should just have all met up for dinner at someone's house. I guess it was interesting to be back in the high school after all these years, but aside from that, we'd probably have visited with each other more over a meal."

Myrtle clucked. "Then poor Belinda's death. What a horrid thing. Did you stay in touch with her over the years?"

"No. No, I didn't," said Evie tightly.

"What about Harold?"

"Certainly not," said Evie. "Harold and Belinda had nothing in common."

Myrtle wondered if Evie protested too much. "Really? I thought I spotted them catching up at the reunion. During that ill-fated scavenger hunt."

"You must have been mistaken," said Evie stiffly.

"You were with them. Don't you remember?"

Evie gave a quick shake of her head. Myrtle studied her. Was she trying to cover up something? Or was she genuinely forgetful? Regardless, she wasn't going to admit to anything, so it was best to move on. After all, if Evie wasn't happy, she'd just hop in her car and go.

"I understand you were a teacher, too," said Myrtle.

Evie brightened at this. "That's right. Thirty-five years in elementary school. It was truly wonderful. I do miss teaching, don't you?"

Myrtle didn't, actually. She'd liked the kids just fine, but she hadn't been fond of the red tape she often encountered, the meager pay, and the endless staff meetings. But she nodded her head in agreement.

"You and Harold have been married a long while," said Myrtle.

"Yes. It was a struggle when we were just starting out, you know. Not much money and we were both so tired at the end of the day. But things improve with time, don't they?" Then Evie colored, as if suspecting she'd been insensitive. "Sorry, Myrtle. I remember you lost Stanley early. You probably found that things *didn't* improve with time."

"Well, they did and they didn't. Losing Stanley was a blow, of course. But I've had good friends, good family. All in all, life has been good."

Evie nodded, but her eyes were dark. Myrtle wondered if Harold and Evie were quite as happy as Evie was making out.

"I suppose you don't have any thoughts on who might have murdered Belinda?" asked Myrtle.

"Are the police absolutely sure it was murder?"

"Absolutely," said Myrtle. "It certainly wasn't an accident. And Belinda didn't strike herself on the head, you know."

"No, I suppose not." Evie looked resigned. "I just can't believe someone from our high school class killed Belinda."

"It's an uncomfortable truth, isn't it? But people do get fired up, you know. And when they do, sometimes they don't think. This seems like the kind of murder where it was very spontaneous. Spur-of-the-moment. It's not as if one of our former classmates is a criminal mastermind."

Evie seemed slightly more cheerful at this. "That's true. Otherwise, they'd have spent the last sixty-seven years in prison, wouldn't they?"

"If they were career criminals? I'd imagine so," said Myrtle. She tilted her head to one side. "High school was so long ago, wasn't it? But I do seem to have a faint recollection of Belinda dating Harold at one point."

Evie gave her a cool look. "Only briefly. They didn't work out."

"No, I'm sure you and Harold were a much better match. Belinda always seemed too interested in herself. But she was ambitious, and it would have made sense that she'd have been interested in dating someone who was clearly destined for an excellent profession."

Evie said, "Belinda moved on well, didn't she? She's the kind of person who always lands with her feet on the ground."

Myrtle said, "Were you surprised to get an invitation to the reunion?" She tamped down the irritation she still felt that she hadn't received one.

"Of course. For one thing, it wasn't a reunion year at all. It would have made sense if it were our 65th or 70th. But the 67th? It was very strange."

Myrtle said, "Precisely. But then Belinda brought up that our class was dwindling and it was now or never."

"I suppose. Although I know several people who are one-hundred or older." Evie shrugged. "At any rate, it was odd. Plus, Belinda called us. It wasn't a written invitation."

This did surprise Myrtle. "Belinda doesn't seem the type to do casual invites. I'd have thought she'd have had something engraved."

"That's exactly what I thought. Apparently, she'd done some work to dig up everyone's phone numbers."

Myrtle frowned. "That's very curious. Wouldn't it have been simpler to do an open invitation on social media? Isn't that the way things are done these days?"

"I've no idea. But I can tell you that it was very surprising to hear from Belinda out of the blue like that."

Myrtle asked, "Have you thought about who might have wanted to murder her?"

"I don't even know these people. I barely knew them in high school."

"Naturally," said Myrtle. "Same with me. Still, we're always left with our impressions, aren't we? Ideas that stick with us about people and their motivations."

Evie considered this, but looked ill at ease. Perhaps she didn't want to cast aspersions on her former classmates. Or perhaps she really didn't have any impressions at all. "Maybe Frank?" she offered.

Myrtle began to feel slightly sorry for Frank. It seemed as if everyone suspected either him or Gladys. "What makes you think Frank could have been involved?"

"Oh, nothing. Nothing really. You asked for impressions, Myrtle."

Myrtle changed tack. "Let me ask you something completely different. Remember back to high school." She waited momentarily while Evie's mind traversed many decades. "Do you remember some sort of incident between Millie Thatcher and Belinda? Way back in the day?"

Evie brightened. "I do recollect something. I'd completely forgotten about it, of course, until you mentioned it. Millie couldn't *stand* Belinda and kept saying she'd ruined her life. Do you think she still holds a grudge? After sixty-seven years?"

It seemed incomprehensible to Myrtle. She herself might hold a grudge for a while, but not after she'd enacted some sort of revenge against the hapless person. Like Red getting the gnome treatment. Now that the gnomes were out in her yard, she wasn't at all concerned about Red's irritating behavior. Myrtle said, "Well, it seems like a stretch, doesn't it? But still, the desire to enact vengeance against Belinda might have proven insurmountable when Millie saw Belinda in person for the first time since high school."

Evie nodded enthusiastically, happily latching onto the theory. "Yes, that makes sense. They were both back in the building where it happened. It brought it all back to Millie, and she couldn't help herself. She lashed out at her in the art room during the scavenger hunt."

Myrtle said slowly, "Of course, Millie did seem very intent on *winning* the scavenger hunt."

"But Millie was always an over-achiever. She's the type of person who'd be able to quickly murder someone, then go on and win a competition."

Myrtle thought this was perhaps true. But it also seemed like quite a feat for someone in their mid-eighties. "This disagreement between Millie and Belinda—do you remember what it entailed?"

Evie said, "A little bit, yes. It wasn't something I was interested in. Millie claimed Belinda had taken her research notebook and presented Millie's work as her own at the science fair."

This seemed something of a piddly infraction to Myrtle, at least for murder. As someone who'd worked in the world of academia, if only on the high school level, for many years, plagiarism was serious business. But was it enough to murder over?

Evie must have seen the doubt in Myrtle's eyes. She said, "Don't you remember how angry Millie was?"

Myrtle did, to a certain extent. But Millie also seemed to walk around with a permanent cloud of indignation hovering above her. "What was the science experiment about?"

"Who knows? I do remember it had something to do with plants. That's because Millie was forever in the high school greenhouse and because I found it so surprising that Belinda was showing an interest in botany."

Myrtle said, "I did ask Millie about the conflict she'd had with Belinda in high school. But she acted as if there were no hard feelings between them. As if she didn't remember what I was talking about."

"That's suspicious right there."

Myrtle said, "However, I can't imagine the science fair was such a big deal."

"It clearly was to Millie. Plus, I could imagine it really getting under her skin. After all, Belinda always seemed like she had everything. It wouldn't have seemed fair to Millie that Belinda had looks, popularity, *and* major brainpower. I mean, Belinda was bright, don't get me wrong. But winning a science fair wasn't really in Belinda's wheelhouse."

Then Evie effectively shut down further talk about the reunion or Belinda. Instead, she chatted with single-minded determination on the topics of pets, Medicare, and gardening until Myrtle was delighted when Evie finally stated it was time for her to leave.

Chapter Thirteen

After Evie's visit, Myrtle decided to take a break. Her mind was whirling, and she needed it to shut down just a little. Ordinarily, she'd accomplish this by watching her soap opera. She did, however, want to wait and watch it with Miles. Instead, she picked up her crossword puzzle book. Myrtle did, in fact, have many such books. She suspected Red and Elaine were stumped on what to give her for Christmas and her birthday. Myrtle sympathized with them. After all, Myrtle didn't really need many things.

It was six o'clock when her doorbell rang again. Myrtle was about to sneak to the side window and peer out to make sure it wasn't Erma Sherman on a mission to ruin the remainder of her day. Then she remembered the doorbell app. When she saw Elaine and her darling grandson, Jack, standing there, she hurried over to let them in.

Elaine and Jack beamed at her as she opened the door.

"Nana!" chortled Jack. He hugged Myrtle around her leg.

"How's my favorite grandson?" asked Myrtle. "Would you like to find the toy basket?"

Jack nodded excitedly. But this meant he had to put down the bag he was carrying first. He thrust it at his grandmother before trotting over to the toy closet and pulling out the basket of toys.

Myrtle peeked into the bag. It was completely full of toothbrushes.

Elaine smiled proudly at her. "Those are for you! I don't know if I told you the last time we spoke, but I have a friend who's big into couponing."

Myrtle quickly saw where this was heading. Elaine was constantly embroiled in new hobbies. It was, Myrtle supposed, admirable that she was interested in expanding her horizons and exploring new things. However, it was unfortunate that the hobbies inevitably went poorly. Often, Myrtle found herself having to bestow praise on some horrid painting or wretched sculpture. If her new hobby was couponing, Myrtle guessed it was better than some alternatives.

"That's very kind of you to bring the toothbrushes," said Myrtle. Although, at the rate she used toothbrushes, the number she just received might last her until the end of her days.

Elaine also had a bag with her, a rather large one. "I have a few other things for you. Want me to set them down in your bathroom?"

Now Myrtle suspected that she might have enough toothbrushes to last several lifetimes. If more were in Elaine's heavy bag. "That would be great, but could I see what's inside?"

Elaine beamed at her. "Sure! Take a look."

Myrtle peered inside to find many mouthwashes and dental flosses. "Do I have a problem with my breath that you're trying to subtly tell me about?"

"No, no. These are the spoils of my couponing. It's almost like a game, Myrtle. Those toothbrushes were only two cents."

"Two cents apiece?"

Elaine shook her head with a big grin on her face. "No! Just two cents, total."

"Elaine, you seem quite giddy. Should you perhaps sit down for a minute?"

Jack came over to them, carrying a truck from the toy basket. "Fort," he said solemnly.

"Yes, we should show Nana your fort, shouldn't we?" Elaine looked at Myrtle and said, "As long as we're not interrupting anything. I should have asked before we barged in here."

"You and Jack are *never* interrupting anything. Red is another story." Myrtle reached out and held Jack's hand. "Now I'd love to see that fort. It must be pretty amazing."

Jack nodded happily as they set off across the street to their house. "Fort!"

Elaine looked just slightly uneasy. "We probably need to watch our step, that's all. The fort is rather sprawling. And there are a bunch of other things surrounding it."

"Not a problem. I have my cane in one hand and Jack in the other. And I feel particularly surefooted today."

As they walked down their driveway, Myrtle said, "Actually, I've noticed you've been parking your van in the driveway, Elaine. That's a bit unusual, isn't it? Red's cruiser is always in the driveway, but you're usually in the garage."

Elaine laughed. "Observant as usual."

Jack pointed to the garage. "Fort!"

And indeed, when Elaine hit the garage door opener, the door rolled up to reveal a tremendous fort made entirely of paper towels, some in bulk, some individual, all encased in plastic. Which was good, because they were in a garage. Garages weren't known for their sterile environments.

Jack looked up at his grandmother for approval.

"It's a wonderful fort," said Myrtle a little weakly. It was quite a stunning edifice. And around Jack's fort were many other goods. Shampoo, deodorants and toilet paper stretched as far as the eye could see. She understood why Elaine was no longer parking in the garage.

"Let me show you my coupon command center," said Elaine, reaching for a large binder on an overloaded shelf.

"Are you preparing for the apocalypse?" asked Myrtle, looking around her.

"Hmm? Oh, ha! No, not doing that. Just so you know, I'm going to be donating most of this to the women's shelter. And the food to the food pantry."

"There's food, too?" Myrtle peered more closely at Jack's fort.

"Yes, but inside. I decided I didn't really need a dining room right now. You won't believe how many cereals and canned goods I have in there. I'm going to be giving you and Miles both a lot of it, too."

Myrtle gave her a small smile. "What does Red think of your couponing?" Red was ordinarily very unhappy with Elaine's hobbies, mostly because they tended to affect him negatively.

However, he wisely kept his opinion under wraps, not wanting to upset Elaine.

"Well, he was a little funny about the garage at first. But then I explained to him that everything coming into the house and garage is going to head back out again. Or most of it. That made him happier."

Myrtle was certain Red was relieved to hear it. You never really knew quite what direction Elaine's hobbies were going to go in.

Elaine happily showed Myrtle her command center binder, full of printed spreadsheets. The coupons were carefully filed by category.

"I can't imagine the amount of time it must have taken you to cut these coupons out," said Myrtle. "And the shopping on top of it."

"Oh, it's not bad at all. You'll never guess who has the dexterity to cut them out alongside me."

Myrtle said, "Jack, naturally. He's a genius."

"At any rate, he's excellent with a pair of safety scissors." Elaine gave Myrtle an earnest look, and Myrtle had the sudden feeling she was about to be evangelized to. "You know, there is a fantastic deal at the Piggly Wiggly. I could drive you there. I have extra coupons."

"The deal isn't for toothbrushes, is it?"

"No, it's for butter. The butter will practically be free after the coupon savings," said Elaine.

Myrtle considered her butter situation. The fact of the matter was that she only really used butter when she ate toast. Or when she was making casseroles, which she only did after someone died. And, although Belinda had most certainly died, there was no grieving soul who required a homemade casserole in this particular instance.

"I might pass on the butter, dear. I do appreciate it. But I don't think I need it. And even paying a few cents for something I don't need is out of my budget."

Elaine looked a bit disappointed, but nodded approvingly. "That's what they warn us about online. Don't get into a spending hole because something is cheap."

Myrtle glanced around the garage, which had every appearance of a spending hole.

Elaine said, "Want to see the dining room? I have a few things I want to give you."

Elaine seemed so very ardent that Myrtle didn't have the heart to turn her down again.

"Sure, let's take a look at your dining room."

Jack skipped ahead of them, then carefully paused before approaching the door to the dining room. Myrtle saw the wisdom in this when she spotted it. It was a warren of cans and boxes of food.

Elaine said, "Yes, maybe it's a good idea if you just look at the dining room from the outside. It can be a little tricky walking around in there. I just know my way around."

"Elaine, when did you start doing this? From what I see, it would have taken years to stockpile this. You're ready for World War III."

"It didn't take nearly as long as you think. I bought in bulk, when I could. Sometimes the store sets a limit on what you can buy, but sometimes not!" Elaine was now rummaging through items, putting things in a bag. "Let's see. Do you eat oatmeal?"

"I'm really more of a grits eater."

Elaine nodded. "Yes, that's right. I think the grits are over here."

Despite the large amount of food, it did seem remarkably organized. And Myrtle was relieved to see Jack's caution regarding the dining room. But then, as she'd observed earlier, he was a genius.

Elaine walked out of the dining room with a tote bag full of food items. "I'll carry it across the street for you."

Myrtle reached for it, testing the weight. "No, it's just fine—not too heavy. Thank you, Elaine."

"I'll come back by soon with more goodies. And give Miles a heads-up that I'll be heading his way, too. What's in store for the rest of your day? Want to join us for supper?"

But Myrtle felt as if maybe she'd rather return to her crossword puzzle book, much as she loved Jack and enjoyed visiting with Elaine. It had been rather hectic recently, after all. "I think I might take my party favor and head on back to the house, if it's all right."

"Of course," said Elaine, giving her a hug. Jack quickly did the same. "Just let me know if you change your mind later."

But later on, Myrtle found herself gently nodding off over an animal documentary featuring warthogs. And soon, she was fast asleep.

The bad thing about falling asleep early was the repercussion the following morning. Myrtle woke up at the ungodly hour of three o'clock. She wondered if her fellow insomniac, Miles, might also be awake and in need of company. Myrtle told herself it was the responsible thing to do, as a friend, to check on Miles.

She put on her robe and her sturdiest slippers and walked outside. It was, as expected, extremely quiet. Then something darted by her feet. Looking closely, she saw it was Pasha. "Darling Pasha! Coming with me to visit Miles?"

Pasha gave her a regretful blink of her eyes before dashing past to follow whatever poor creature she was hunting. Myrtle only hoped the animal wouldn't end up in sections on her front doorstep.

Myrtle smiled as she approached Miles's house. It seemed every light in his home was turned on. She rapped on his front door, which Miles opened right away. "I sort of thought you might show up," he said. "I made coffee."

They settled into Miles's kitchen with their coffees.

"Apparently, I'm extremely predictable," said Myrtle. She wasn't sure whether this peeved her, or whether it was comforting to have a friend who knew her so well.

Miles shrugged. "It tends to happen during these murder investigations. And I was thinking about the case, too. What happened after we spoke with Millie?"

"I decided to invite Evie Blackwood over for a girl's chat."

Miles raised his eyebrows. "Did she come?"

"She did. It might have been pure curiosity that drove her. After all, she and I hadn't been friends back in school. Evie might have simply wondered what I was like now. I didn't really speak to her at the reunion, either."

Miles said, "Did you learn anything?"

"Oh, I don't know. Some odds and ends. For one thing, Belinda actually went to the trouble of calling my former classmates to invite them to the reunion. She didn't mail anything out or post it on social media and tag everyone. It seems to me as if she was picking and choosing who she wanted there."

Miles decided not to comment on this one way or another. It was sore subject for Myrtle.

Myrtle continued, "I wonder if Belinda didn't want me there because she knew I investigate crimes."

"Informally," pointed out Miles.

"Yes. But it's reported in the newspaper and sometimes picked up on the wire. So it's hardly a secret."

Miles said, "So you think perhaps Belinda had some sort of agenda for the reunion."

"I do. I think she invited particular people to come. And she wanted to get those people aside to talk to them about something. Then one of my former classmates decided they weren't pleased by whatever Belinda was saying. They killed her because of it."

Miles said, "I suppose you could test your theory a little. The picking-and-choosing part, anyway. Go online and look up your classmates. See if they're still alive and kicking. Then ask them if they received any sort of invitation to the event."

Myrtle made a face. "That sounds rather laborious. And I'd have to reach out to people I actively disliked in high school. They likely haven't improved with time. But I'll think about it."

"Did you learn anything else from Evie?"

Myrtle nodded. "There was this incident between Millie Thatcher and Belinda in high school. I recalled there was some sort of fracas, but I couldn't remember exactly what it was about, although I thought I remembered something about research. When I asked Evie about it, she told me it was because Belinda had stolen Millie's idea for a science fair competition. Apparently, this was a huge deal, at least to Millie."

"Plagiarism would be very upsetting," said Miles. "It's theft of one's intellectual property."

"Are you *sure* you were an engineer? Sometimes you sound rather like a lawyer."

Miles sighed. "Anyway, was there a reason why Millie would have taken this theft so personally? A science fair seems like small potatoes to me."

"It did to me, too, but Evie intimated that it wasn't. That it was devastating to Millie. That Millie stated Belinda had ruined her life."

Miles said, "That sounds very melodramatic. Like the sort of thing someone would say when they were very young."

"Agreed. Although maybe, at that point in one's life, it *does* make a difference. Maybe Millie lost the chance to attend a better university or get on a particular track for her life. Who knows? It certainly sounds like a motive, at any rate."

"How did Evie act when you were basically interrogating her during your girls' chat?" asked Miles.

"She did try to change the subject back to gardening or Medicare or whatever topic didn't involve murder."

Miles said, "Perhaps that's only natural. Talking about murder isn't exactly relaxing."

"Most people seem to love talking about murder. It's a gossipy thing to do. It wasn't only that. Evie also claimed Harold and Belinda didn't talk during the reunion. But I clearly saw them myself, so Evie was obviously lying. She also seemed defensive when talking about Belinda and Harold's old relationship in high school. I remember there definitely being history there. Basically, Evie was evasive."

Miles nodded. "Well, it sounds like you learned quite a bit."

"Yes. And there was something else I learned yesterday. Elaine is on a shopping bender."

"That doesn't sound like Elaine," said Miles, frowning.

"It's a new hobby. I should have prefaced that by saying that she's couponing. So the shopping bender isn't costing much money. But now she has turned her dining room and garage into a warehouse full of stuff."

Miles considered this. "It doesn't sound as bad as some of her other hobbies. It sounds like the kind of hobby she could excel at, for one. And it wouldn't intersect with us and our lives very much."

"Sadly, she's passing on the spoils of her battles. She gave me more toothbrushes than I can conceivably use in this lifetime. And Elaine plans on foisting things on you, too."

Miles sighed. "That sounds like you and I will have to donate extras to the food pantry. And Goodwill, I guess, although I'm not sure if they take toothbrushes."

"Fortunately, she *is* going to donate most extras to a women's shelter, so that's helpful. And I guess it keeps her busy." Myrtle looked at the clock. "I was going to suggest that we go to Bo's Diner for breakfast. But somehow, it still appears to be the middle of the night."

"We should kill some time, then. Chess?"

Myrtle was surprised that Miles would suggest playing chess with her. Although she couldn't seem to remember the names of the pieces, she did somehow have a knack for the game. It did irritate him to lose so often. And she didn't feel like letting him win. "How about cards instead? We could invite Wanda over. She loves cards and she can drive herself down here now, with the new car."

"New, used car," said Miles. "And I believe Wanda has too much sense to be awake at this time of the night."

Which was just when there was a knock at the door. Myrtle and Miles looked at each other. Then Miles walked over to peer out his front window. He turned. "It's . . ."

"Yes, Wanda."

Chapter Fourteen

He opened the door wide for Wanda, who gave him a gap-toothed smile. "Hi there," she said. "Playin' cards?"

Myrtle said, "Yes, and thank goodness you're here. With only two players, Miles and I would have been stuck playing go fish or old maid. Now that you're joining us, I think hearts are in order."

Wanda beamed at this. She was particularly fond of playing hearts and seemed to have a lucky streak going.

"Coffee?" asked Miles. "There's a cup's worth left, and then I'll make another pot."

Wanda followed him into the kitchen while Myrtle took the deck of cards from Miles's bookshelf and started dealing them. Minutes later, they started playing the game while the TV played an animal documentary, fortunately *not* one featuring warthogs.

This time, they each won a hand at hearts, which was all very equable. Since it's a game of both chance and skill, everyone had even footing. Myrtle did have one horrible hand where she was saddled with a bunch of hearts and the queen of spades, but not enough bad cards to "shoot the moon" and win the hand. However, she somehow ended up winning the game, possibly because everyone else ended up with terrible cards the next time.

Somehow, between nature documentaries and cards, the time passed quickly. Myrtle looked at the clock again to find it was time to head to the diner. Then she looked down at herself and realized she was still in her robe and slippers. "Fiddlesticks," she said.

Miles said, "Why don't you go home and change, and then Wanda and I will come by with my car?"

"I'll just walk back when I'm ready, and we'll leave from here."

Wanda added ominously, "Might be a minute before we git to th' diner, ennyway."

Myrtle said, "Well, that sounds foreboding. All right, I'll head back home and will be ready in a couple of minutes."

Soon, they were heading the short distance to downtown and the diner. Wanda still seemed uneasy from the backseat, fidgeting as if she couldn't sit still.

"Everything okay?" asked Myrtle.

"Nope," grated Wanda. "I reckon we should run by th' high school."

"That place again?" Myrtle turned to look at Wanda. "There's not another body, is there?"

Wanda just looked at her grimly.

Miles looked even grimmer. "It sounds as if we should actually stay away from the high school altogether. We should call the police and then go to the diner and have breakfast."

His voice was quite earnest, as if by speaking the words, he could make them come true. Myrtle rained on his parade, however. "You know I can't call Red and tell him Wanda has a funny feeling about the high school. He's looking for any excuse to lock me away in Greener Pastures Retirement Home."

So, to Miles's dismay, they took a detour to the high school. Miles pulled into a parking spot in the front of the building, but Wanda was already shaking her head. "In th' back."

Miles drove slowly to the back of the school, where the football field was surrounded by a track. And on that track, they saw a woman lying on the ground.

Chapter Fifteen

It only took a minute for Miles to hurry down the stadium stairs to the track. Wanda was in less of a hurry, looking more mournful than worried. Myrtle, hindered a bit by her cane, brought up the rear.

Miles had checked for a pulse and, finding none, stood slowly up, shaking his head. "Do you know who this is?" he asked Myrtle.

"Unfortunately, it's Evie, Harold's wife. Heavens. What's she doing out here?"

Miles said, "We need to call Red and let him know."

Myrtle knew they should. She was also hesitant to do it. When Red arrived at a crime scene, it tended to put a damper on any investigating she might be doing herself. But Miles was already dialing Red's number.

Myrtle turned to Evie. She was wearing sensible clothes, the kind of clothes one should be wearing when exercising. It was very early, but not too early to be walking around a track, if one was the sort who enjoyed getting physical activity early. It looked as if Evie hadn't brought anything with her, aside from her cane, which lay a few feet away.

The track was that rubbery sort of material that tended to be easier on joints than concrete. But Evie wasn't technically on the track, but on the grass next to it. That seemed odd. If someone was setting out to exercise on a track, presumably they'd be on the track.

"Footprints," said Wanda, pointing to some marks in the grass, still wet with dew.

Myrtle took a picture of them with her phone. "I'm not really sure what I'm looking at, but the prints are helpful to have." She looked down at Evie. "Considering her head wound, it sure doesn't look like this was an accident."

"She couldn't have hit her head when she fell down?" asked Miles. Murder still made him a bit squeamish. Particularly in the early morning.

"I think that's what the killer wanted us to think. See how her cane is positioned? But the cane is too far away. When you fall, the cane would usually end up underneath you, surely. Not a few feet away. And the head injury is on her side. She's lying on her back, so how would that have happened?"

The sound of a car entering the school's parking lot made Myrtle sigh. "Red's here, I suppose. How annoying."

But it wasn't Red at all. It was Detective Shaw. Myrtle sighed again. "I suppose I'm about to be subjected to interrogation again."

"I get the feeling you secretly enjoy being thought a murderer," said Miles. He and Wanda shared a grin.

"Certainly not," said Myrtle.

Shaw strode toward them, his thin mustache twitching with suspicion. "Mrs. Clover. What an extraordinary coincidence to find you at another murder scene."

"Is it? Bradley is rife with murder."

Shaw said in a pointed manner, "And you always end up discovering the bodies."

"Not always. Sometimes I'm on the scene after they've already been located," said Myrtle with a sniff.

"You were present at Belinda Holloway's murder."

"I was covering the reunion for the paper," said Myrtle coldly. "As you well know."

"And now you're here with Evie Blackwood. Who is apparently quite dead."

"Very observant of you, Shaw. I can see how you made it to the detective rank," said Myrtle. "But I wasn't here because I was murdering poor Evie. I was on my way to breakfast." She glanced over at Wanda. If she said Wanda had suggested a trip by the high school and told Shaw that Wanda had a gift, she was sure the simpleton would decide to interrogate Wanda. Better left unmentioned.

Shaw raised an eyebrow. "Breakfast? I wasn't aware Bradley High offered breakfast food in July. Or for non-students."

Myrtle straightened to her full height of nearly six feet and looked coolly at Shaw. "On the way to breakfast, I suddenly felt quite nostalgic. I wanted to show Miles the school where I'd been both a student and a teacher. Miles isn't from around here."

Shaw looked suspiciously at Miles. "I don't believe I've met you." He turned to Wanda. "Or you."

Miles cleared his throat. "I'm Miles. I'm originally from Atlanta."

"Wanda," said Wanda.

"Okay," said Shaw. "I have to say it seems very early in the morning for anyone to be skulking around the high school."

"We're sensible people," said Myrtle. "Sensible people do things early in the morning during a Southern July."

"It's very hot," agreed Miles. He was perspiring, which made him seem even more earnest and believable. But then, he was a good sidekick.

Wanda was keeping quiet. She looked a bit on edge.

"At six-thirty in the morning?" Shaw's eyes narrowed.

"I'm elderly. We wake up early. In fact, the three of us have been playing cards for hours."

This didn't seem to convince Shaw of their innocence.

"For heaven's sake," said Myrtle. "Are you suggesting I'm patrolling Bradley looking for corpses?"

"I'm suggesting you might be *responsible* for the corpses," said Shaw.

"Nothing could be farther from the truth. I have better things to do with my time."

Shaw took out a small notebook. "Such as?"

"Crosswords, reading the newspaper, watching soap operas, and avoiding irritating people."

Shaw carefully wrote this down, which both amused and irritated Myrtle. "And where were you last night, Mrs. Clover? Driving around?"

"I don't have a car, detective. I was watching a documentary on warthogs with my feral cat, aside from sleeping."

Myrtle's answer seemed to stump Shaw momentarily. It wasn't clear if it was because of the mention of warthogs or feral cats. He paused. "Mrs. Clover, I don't think you appreciate the gravity of this situation."

Myrtle heard Red's cruiser pulling into the parking lot and felt an uncommon feeling of relief at her son's approach. "On the contrary, I appreciate it very much. However, I don't appreciate being treated like a serial killer simply for living in a town where the occasional murder happens."

"Frequently happens," corrected Shaw.

"Surely that's Red's problem and not mine," said Myrtle coldly.

Red came hurrying down the slope to the track, foregoing the stairs in his haste. On his heels were the state police.

"Mama, what are you doing here? And with Miles and Wanda?" Red asked.

"That's exactly what I've been trying to get to the bottom of," said Shaw.

"Hi Red," said Miles meekly.

Myrtle was in no mood to be meek, however. "Shaw seems to believe I'm depraved."

"Mama isn't depraved," Red assured the lieutenant. "However, there are many other unpleasant words to describe her."

It made Myrtle very happy to consider her gnomes staring out across the street from Red's house. Perhaps she'd have Dusty come back and completely empty the shed, putting all of her yard ornaments outside. Especially her new favorite, the giant gnome.

Red made a shooing motion to his mother and politely said to Miles, "Maybe the three of you could wait in your vehicle? We might have more questions."

Miles nodded, and Wanda and Myrtle followed him to the car. They'd nearly reached Miles's sedan when Myrtle stopped. "That's Harold Blackwood walking up."

Miles said, "Oh no."

"Don't be melodramatic, Miles. We'll have to keep him from going down to that track and seeing Evie. It's much better to be the ones who kindly inform him."

Miles said, "I'm not sure you're the best emissary from our group to tell Harold his wife of many years has been murdered."

"Wanda, then?"

Wanda gave them a leery look. "Don't know 'im."

"True. At least he's met Miles at the diner," said Myrtle.

Miles was looking uncomfortable.

"Well, it's either you or me," said Myrtle.

Miles squared his shoulders, looking as if he was about to be greeted by his firing squad.

Myrtle thought Harold looked a little lost as he joined them. "Have you seen Evie, Myrtle? She took the car from the hotel, saying she was going to take a walk. But she should have come back by now."

"What time did she leave for the walk?" asked Myrtle.

"Six-thirty. She likes walking right at dawn, before it gets too hot. I just walked here from the hotel."

It was not an insignificant amount to walk. Perhaps Harold was in better shape than most octogenarians, despite his use of a cane.

Miles looked as if he were in an agony of indecision on how to deliver the terrible news. Myrtle gave him a hard stare while Wanda just looked worried.

"Harold," he said. Then he stopped. "Harold." Miles glanced over at Myrtle, panicked.

Myrtle sighed. "What Miles is trying to say is that we have some bad news. Why don't you have a seat?" She gestured to the passenger side of Miles's front seat.

Harold stiffened, then shook his head. "I don't want to sit down."

Myrtle said, "Evie was murdered on the track. We're all very sorry." She looked to Miles to see how her delivery had done on the sensitivity meter. He gave her a small nod of approval.

Now Harold looked very much as if he'd wished he'd taken a seat after all. He swayed just slightly on his feet, leaning hard on the cane.

Miles, perhaps not wanting to scoop Harold off the parking lot pavement, swiftly opened the car door and gently ushered Harold into the seat.

"How?" he asked.

Myrtle said carefully, "I'm sure she didn't suffer. It was clearly foul play, but it must have been sudden." She didn't feel like spelling out the cause of death in case Red berated her for it later. He didn't know she was questioning his suspect in the parking lot. This reminded her that her time was limited for asking questions before Red came up and ruined it all.

"We need to find out who did this to Evie," said Myrtle.

"Yes," said Harold with alacrity. "Evie, of all people. She didn't deserve to die. She was a good person."

Myrtle noted Harold hadn't said that Belinda was a good person who didn't deserve to die. But then, no one had. Belinda had some hard edges.

"How was Evie yesterday and today?" she asked. "Did it seem like she had anything on her mind? Did she mention being worried about something?"

Harold frowned at Myrtle. "I should ask you the same thing. You saw Evie yesterday afternoon."

"I did, yes. I felt as if it might be nice for Evie and I to catch up. And it was. It was lovely." It hadn't been, but there was no need to bother Harold with that.

Harold's frown deepened. "And what are the three of you doing over here in the first place? Did you discover Evie?"

It sounded a bit far-fetched to say they'd been on their way to the diner when their psychic friend said they should go to the high school. So Myrtle used the same line she'd used with Shaw. "We were on our way to breakfast, then I wanted to show Wanda and Miles the high school where I'd spent so many happy years."

Harold looked unsure, but ultimately appeared to accept this rather odd explanation. "You found her, then?"

Myrtle nodded, and Harold gave a trembly sigh. Then he said, "You asked what her demeanor was like yesterday and today. Yes, I think she had something on her mind. She didn't share it with me, though. I thought perhaps Belinda's death and our own imminent mortality was weighing on her."

"Tell me what happened this morning," said Myrtle. It was a pushier question than usual, but the fact of the matter was that

Red was going to come stomping up to the parking lot at any moment and ruin everything.

Harold nodded. "I don't think Evie was sleeping well. She was restless last night, at any rate. But then, we're sleeping in a hotel. We're used to our mattress at home, of course. And sleeping in a hotel is noisy sometimes. The icemaker is always going off, the elevator arriving at the floor is loud. I hadn't slept well either, but I'd fallen into a heavy sleep around two o'clock this morning."

Myrtle always wondered what a heavy sleep might feel like. What was it like to fall asleep and have no knowledge of anything for hours? She was such a light sleeper that even if she *was* asleep, the sound of her air conditioning turning off and on could wake her up. "So you were asleep when Evie left?"

Harold nodded. "She woke me up to tell me she was heading out in the car for the track. I fell right back asleep again. Like I said, she loves walking for exercise and always wants to beat the summer heat. So the fact that she wanted to take a walk wasn't surprising."

"But then she didn't come back when you expected."

"Right," said Harold. He suddenly looked emotional, and Myrtle worried he might suddenly start crying. She did so hate tears. She was about to rummage in her large purse to find her pack of tissues when he appeared to get control of himself. He said, "When I woke up, I expected she would be back in the hotel room. Taking a shower, perhaps. Or maybe downstairs, eating breakfast. I looked everywhere. She wasn't answering her phone, which is most unusual. And Evie had taken the car of course, so I set out on foot as soon as possible." He stared toward the track. "I can't believe this has happened. You're *sure*?"

"I'm sorry, but we're certain. You're sure Evie didn't confide in you? Tell you what was on her mind?" asked Myrtle.

Harold shook his head, then looked uneasy. "I don't think so, no. But then, as I believe I told you earlier, my memory has been a little flaky lately."

"Last time, you mentioned Gladys as a suspect in Belinda's death. Do you feel the same about Evie's death?"

Harold sighed. "I don't know. I can hardly even wrap my head around the fact that this has happened." He paused. "Millie called Evie yesterday."

"What did she say?" asked Myrtle.

Harold paused. "I think she wanted to meet up with Evie to walk this morning. Yes, that was it. She likes walking in the mornings and found out Evie does, too. She wanted to walk the track with her." He frowned. "I thought it was weird at the time. Maybe Millie has changed a lot, I don't know."

Miles asked, "Changed how?"

Harold said, "When we were back in school together, Millie wasn't a morning person, at all. As hard-working, smart, driven, and dedicated as she was, she still struggled to get to school on time in the mornings."

Myrtle frowned, too. "I suppose people can change." But being a morning or a night person seemed like something people were wired with. It seemed somehow integral to one's biological clock. Did that ever change all that much?

Harold continued, "Also, I don't remember Millie Thatcher and Evie being friends . . . ever. They were always competing in school. Anyway, that's all I know about that."

Myrtle, Miles, and Wanda exchanged a look. If Millie had been at the track, she had either left without reporting the murder, or she might have been the murderer herself.

But suddenly, Red was upon them. He was red in the face, irritated at the sight of his mother with Harold.

Chapter Sixteen

"You told me to wait at the car," said Myrtle sweetly. "Then Harold happened up on foot."

Red's voice was tight. "You've informed him, then."

Harold broke in. "I was on my way down to the track. Your mother stopped me from going down there. To do that, she had to tell me what was going on."

Red nodded reluctantly at the logic of this. But he appeared unwilling to grant her the opportunity to stick around and encounter even more suspects. "Let's have the three of you head home now," he said. "I'll catch up with you if I need to ask more questions."

"We were going to the diner, not home," said Myrtle.

"Fine. Anywhere but here." Then he turned to speak with Harold, gesturing for him to take a seat on a bench not too far away, near the entrance of the high school.

Myrtle, Miles, and Wanda climbed into the car. "Mercy," said Myrtle. "What a start to the day."

Miles said, "Wanda, did you know something like that was going to happen?"

"None of this is Wanda's fault, Miles!" said Myrtle with annoyance.

"No, no, of course not," said Miles quickly. "I was just wondering if she had an idea what we were going to encounter on the track."

Wanda was quiet for a second. Then she said, "I knew somethin' wuz wrong. That's all. Somethin' bad."

"Of course you did. And I'm glad you told us to make that detour."

Wanda gave her an apologetic look. "Didn't want yew to haveta lie to them cops."

"Pish. Who cares about that? Since Shaw is an idiot, I figured he'd be suspicious that my gifted friend realized something was wrong. From what I know about Shaw, that would have put you on top of the suspect list, Wanda."

"Yep," she agreed.

Miles said, "Well, what do we make of this new development? Evie's death."

"Let's discuss it over breakfast. I'm famished now. We've been up for hours and hours. I'll think better when I have something in my stomach."

So, minutes later, over biscuits, omelets, grits, and Miles's sad bowl of oatmeal, Myrtle said, "Back to Evie's death." She glanced suspiciously around her, as if someone might be trying to listen in. But no one seemed in the slightest bit interested and were involved in their own conversations. Still, Myrtle lowered her voice. "Harold seemed to think Millie Thatcher was responsible."

"Our resident expert on *A Tale of Two Cities*," said Miles morosely. "Somehow, I don't like to think of a Charles Dickens enthusiast as a crazed killer."

"No one is even saying this killer is crazed. Depraved, perhaps. But they might be in full use of their faculties. So perhaps Millie killed Belinda and Evie became suspicious for some reason. Maybe Evie saw or heard something."

Miles said, "Then why would Evie go for a walk with Millie? Wouldn't she have been scared of her? Avoided her? Spoken to the police?"

Wanda drawled, "Mebbe she wudn't sure of whut she saw."

"Good point, Wanda!" said Myrtle. "Evie might have had questions about what she saw. Maybe Evie thought she might be misinterpreting something and wanted to clear it up with Millie face-to-face. Otherwise, she'd be throwing her under the bus if she called the police."

"Still, it seems like an ill-advised time to meet with a potential murderer," said Miles. "Dawn? At a deserted high school in July?"

"Maybe Evie had an inflated sense of safety. Maybe she thought she and Millie were friends and that Millie wouldn't hurt her," offered Myrtle.

"From what Harold just told us, Millie and Evie were never friendly," said Miles.

"Well, somebody killed Evie, and it wasn't me, despite what Shaw might think." Myrtle sighed. "I wish we had Lieutenant Perkins back. I do miss his common sense."

Wanda looked at an ancient Timex watch hanging on her thin wrist. She gave them an apologetic look. "I gotta go. Gotta meetin' with Lady Cassandra."

"She certainly pays rather better for your company than Miles and I do. You should have stopped us from dilly-dallying over breakfast, especially since you have a long drive ahead of you."

Miles, as he often did, quickly paid for everyone's breakfast, and they headed off in his car back to Myrtle's, where Wanda's vehicle was waiting for her.

Myrtle suddenly said, "I don't want to hold you up, but by any chance might you need toothbrushes, Wanda?"

Wanda gave her a snaggle-toothed grin. "Reckon I could. Figured yew might ask me."

Myrtle hurried inside, stuck a handful of individually packaged toothbrushes in a plastic grocery bag, and came outside again, thrusting them at Wanda. Wanda gave them both a smile and a wave and set off slowly for home.

Myrtle's phone chirped at her. "It's Gladys. Apparently, that informal memorial service the group was proposing is going to be right after lunch." She scowled. "At the high school gymnasium."

"That seems a bit macabre," said Miles. "Considering recent events."

"I suppose no one really knows about Evie's death, aside from Harold. But it's bad enough that it's being held where Belinda lived her final moments." Myrtle paused. "I suppose I should bring something. Food or some such. That's what one does during these occasions."

"Is it?" asked Miles. "I don't believe we've ever brought food to a memorial service. Only to grieving families' houses."

"Gracious, Miles. Your tone! You'd think I was planning on bringing a bomb to the memorial service. And don't be pedantic. The only reason we don't usually bring food to memorial services is because they ordinarily have food there. This one is going to be some half-baked function. Food might be the only good thing about it."

Miles looked as if he very much doubted this. "How about if we go to the Piggly Wiggly and pick up some ready-made cookies? They make good cookies at their bakery."

"After Elaine gave me all that food? That seems rather wasteful. I'm sure I can pull something together with what I have. I believe there were boxes and boxes of Jell-O. Food involves creativity, after all." Myrtle paused. "And I think you should attend the memorial service with me."

"Absolutely not," said Miles swiftly. His answer might have had something to do with being associated with Myrtle's makeshift food plans.

Myrtle scowled at him, but Miles continued, "I didn't know Belinda. This is a small group service of your former classmates, and I won't fit in."

"You always fit in, Miles."

"Not this time," he said. He paused. "What time is this memorial service?"

Myrtle looked at the text again. "1:00."

"Will that be enough time for the Jell-O to set?"

Myrtle said, "Close enough. Don't be so fretful, Miles! Everything will be fine."

Suddenly, Miles looked uneasy. "I'm getting a bad feeling about this whole thing. Perhaps I should attend the memorial service, after all."

"Are you getting a premonition? That's very Wanda-esque."

Miles said, "It's not a premonition. It's the fact that the high school has now been the scene of two violent deaths recently."

"Well, I appreciate your protectiveness."

"That's a surprise," said Miles. "You don't care for it when Red's being protective."

"Red's not being protective. He's being controlling. There's quite a difference. Could you pick me up at 12:45? That'll be more than enough time."

Chapter Seventeen

After Miles left, Myrtle decided she likely should tackle the Jell-O, considering the time it took to set (which she couldn't exactly recall, but was sure she had enough time for). Sure enough, Elaine had given her several boxes of the powdery gelatin. Elaine had also put shredded cheese in the fridge. Myrtle knew she'd eaten quite a bit of aspic with cheese on it in the 1970s. She wanted to say it had been made with a soft drink of some sort—perhaps 7-Up. The 1970s were not particularly a decade she wanted to repeat, but it was nice to remember the food she'd enjoyed.

She peered into Elaine's bag of food for more inspiration and saw several cans of fruit cocktail. Myrtle smiled to herself, pulling them out. It was practically a pity to waste such a magnificent salad on her former classmates and at the scene of two murders.

Myrtle peered at the instructions on the back of the box of gelatin. She muttered to herself, "Hot water to dissolve, then cold water." She'd just poured the boiling water over the lime powder when her doorbell app chirped at her.

She suspiciously pulled up the app, sure her luck at evading Erma Sherman was at an end. But it was Elaine with Jack, beaming cheerfully at the doorbell camera. Her arms seemed loaded with bulk purchases.

Myrtle hurried to the door, and Elaine strode through, Jack in her wake. "Look what I bought for practically nothing! Twenty boxes of crackers and fifteen cans of soup. Don't worry, I'm only giving you a fraction of them. The rest is headed to the food pantry."

Again, it looked like far more food than Myrtle would eat in months. But she gave her daughter-in-law a big smile. "Wonderful, Elaine! Aren't you clever?"

Jack handed her a picture he'd made of his grandmother. It was a startling likeness of Myrtle, right down to the poof of her hair standing up like Einstein's. "And you're even *more* clever, Jack."

Jack gave her a hug that warmed her heart.

"Are you cooking?" asked Elaine, an ambivalent look on her face.

"Yes, I'm making Jell-O salad for Belinda's memorial service. Actually, I suppose it'll be a joint memorial service, since it would be tacky to leave Evie out. You did hear about Evie, didn't you?"

Elaine frowned. "I don't think I know an Evie."

"Poor Evie was another casualty this morning. Now the surviving members of my high school class are looking fairly slim indeed."

Elaine's eyes grew large. "*That's* why Red left so early this morning."

"It actually wasn't all that early. I'm assuming he must have stayed up working late last night and was perhaps trying to catch up. Evie was murdered at the high school, too."

Elaine shook her head. "How awful." She paused. "You didn't happen to be on the scene, did you?"

"Heavens no. Well, I wasn't on the scene *during* the murder, anyway. Just afterward, with Wanda and Miles. We were heading to the diner for breakfast and took a quick detour. Anyway, the folks from the reunion are holding a memorial service for Belinda in just a bit. I'm guessing we'll be mentioning Evie, too, once everyone learns about her untimely demise."

Elaine said, "Well, it's very nice of you to bring food." She glanced curiously at the concoction. "Is that fruit cocktail?"

"It is, indeed. Some of your spoils from your grocery expeditions. It's nice to use things, isn't it? Waste not, want not." Myrtle paused and added thoughtfully, "I'm not sure if I added the cold water yet. I know I added the boiling water."

"I'm sure you did," said Elaine helpfully. Then she looked proudly at the couple of rolls of paper towels she'd brought in. "Can you believe these paper towels were only twelve cents a roll?"

"Unbelievable," murmured Myrtle. She was still wondering about the cold water.

By the time Elaine and Jack had left, Myrtle had totally lost the thread in terms of the Jell-O. She decided that she'd better be safe than sorry and add the cold water. But she hadn't figured in that she hadn't drained the fruit cocktail cans before adding the fruit. She threw in shredded cheese, then studied it. It looked very green with the lime Jell-O mix.

She rummaged in the food Elaine had brought over and found a small jar of maraschino cherries. Adding those made for some red streaks in the green that Myrtle found quite artistic-looking. It did look a bit watery, but she supposed that might be due to the fact it needed time to firm up. Still, the wateriness made her dither a bit. She decided a bit of instant pudding mix might thicken it some, so it was thrown in. Then she put the whole thing in the fridge to set.

Miles arrived promptly at 12:45, eyeing the wobbling and watery mold in Myrtle's hands with trepidation. "That's very interesting looking, Myrtle. Is it supposed to be that damp?"

"I'm sure it will taste fine. It's the thought that counts with food, isn't it?"

Miles wasn't at all sure this was the case. However, he'd learned from experience that Myrtle could be touchy when it came to her kitchen creations, so he didn't say a word.

Besides Gladys, Myrtle and Miles were the first to arrive. Gladys had apparently been the brains behind the planning of the memorial service, which concerned Myrtle. Gladys had never had much sense, after all.

Gladys greeted them effusively, "So good of you to come, Myrtle! And who is your gentleman friend? I don't believe I've met him."

"This is Miles Bradford. He's a good friend of mine and was kind enough to drive me over today."

Gladys welcomed him, then said to Myrtle, "You're not driving anymore, then?"

"My son sold my car. But I still have my license, so I'll drive from time to time."

Gladys looked suddenly very smug. It was an unbecoming expression. "I drive all the time. It's a wonderful thing. Very relaxing."

"How nice for you," said Myrtle. "Now, if you'll excuse me, I'm going to show Miles the school. He's not from here originally. We'll be back shortly."

Miles carefully placed the glass dish with the watery Jell-O salad on a table. "This is Myrtle's contribution to the service," he said pointedly.

"How lovely," said Gladys, staring at the concoction in bewilderment. "Is it punch?"

"Of course not," snapped Myrtle. "It's fruit salad."

"I see," said Gladys. "How silly of me."

Miles followed Myrtle out of the gym. She was thumping her cane on the floor in irritation as she left. "That Gladys," she muttered.

"Don't worry about it. She's not the brightest bulb anyway, is she?"

Myrtle said, "She certainly isn't and never was. Anyway, I'll give you the ten-cent tour of the school. Most of the place wasn't around when I was a student here. More of it was here when I was teaching, but that was still a long time ago."

"Lead on," said Miles, who seemed glad for any excuse to escape the vicinity of the Jell-O salad.

Myrtle pointed out a couple of landmarks, then walked to her old classroom. She expected to find the door locked again, but was pleasantly surprised when it opened. "My former classroom," she said fondly, although the room felt quite foreign with the smart board in it and the modern desks lined up. Even the teacher's desk seemed quite different, with its ergonomic design.

"I'm guessing it didn't look like this when you were teaching," said Miles.

"Not at all. I had a blackboard, for one, and lots of chalk." Myrtle looked around her again. "It's almost like it's not the same room." The walls were covered with inspirational posters where she'd had posters of famous authors.

Miles and Myrtle returned to the gymnasium to find that others had arrived for the memorial service. Frank was there, setting up folding chairs in a circle. Behind him, Millie was fussing with photographs of Belinda on a posterboard. Myrtle noticed Harold had not yet arrived.

"This is starting to look like a proper memorial," said Myrtle to Miles. "Although I'm not sure why they chose to hold it at the scene of the crime."

"Maybe it's the only place available on short notice," said Miles.

Frank spotted them and waved. He finished arranging a chair before walking over to greet them. He looked curiously at Miles as if still trying to understand what precisely his relationship to Myrtle was. "Good to see you two, even though the circumstances aren't great."

"Circumstances might perhaps be worse than you suppose. Poor Evie is another casualty."

Frank's face fell. "What?"

"Evie Blackwood was found dead early this morning on the high school track," said Myrtle.

Frank looked stunned. He glanced around the room at the other attendees, all busily engaged in preparation. "Does anyone else know?"

"Considering they're not really looped into local gossip, probably not. But I'm surprised *you* haven't heard, since you're a resident of Bradley," said Myrtle.

Frank shook his head. "Yeah, I was home today, just hanging out. I guess if I'd been running errands, I'd have heard."

"No one texted you about it?"

"Nope," said Frank. He sighed. "Do you think somebody's picking off our high school class one-by-one?"

"Decidedly not. That would be a silly exercise, wouldn't it? No, I'm sure Evie likely knew something about Belinda's death. Something that the killer wanted to keep hidden," said Myrtle.

Frank turned to Miles. "What do you make of all this?"

Miles pondered the question, his wire-rimmed glasses slipping slightly down his nose as he considered Frank's query. "It sounds as if no one is telling the complete truth. Everyone seems to have a fragment of information they're willing to share, but only when it points away from themselves."

Myrtle said impatiently, "Well, suspects lie. We've seen that time and time again. Everyone has their petty little secrets that they don't want the rest of Bradley, North Carolina to know."

Frank said, "How did you two know about Evie? From Red?"

Myrtle snorted. "As if Red would voluntarily provide me with any useful information. No, Miles and I, along with our friend Wanda, found Evie this morning."

Frank's eyes widened. "You found another body? Just like that?"

"Not just like that. We were on our way to breakfast."

Frank said, "But you stopped by the high school first?"

"I don't see that it's any of your business, Frank." Myrtle bristled.

"No, it isn't," said Frank. "It's just a little startling, that's all. Two of our classmates dead, and you finding both of them."

"I wasn't alone when Belinda was found. Winston and Gladys were both present, as you might recall."

"True," said Frank. He looked over his shoulder to where Gladys was hanging photographs. "I think I should help finish setting up. I'll talk to you later."

Miles watched him thoughtfully as he strode away. "He seemed a mite defensive to me."

"I believe he's joining the Myrtle's-a-Serial-Killer club." Myrtle saw someone enter the gym and groaned. "I was hoping Winston had something more important to do today."

"At Greener Pastures? What could be more important?"

Myrtle said, "Maybe he was going to get his pottery back from the kiln, so he could paint it. Or maybe there was a sittercise class that he didn't want to pass up."

Miles chuckled. "But then he'd miss out on his opportunity to woo you."

Myrtle shuddered.

Chapter Eighteen

Winston was wearing another festive bow tie, this one navy with small gold stars. Myrtle moved closer to Miles, hoping Winston would take the hint and not launch another attempt at courtship.

"My fair maiden," he said, lifting Myrtle's hand and giving it a peck. She jerked her hand away. "And the esteemed Milton."

"Miles," said Miles.

"Yes. My apologies. Good to see you both, although under such tragic circumstances."

Myrtle said, "Indeed. Made even more tragic by the death of Evie Blackwood."

Winston's bushy eyebrows shot up. "Not Evie!"

"I'm afraid so."

"What on earth happened? Heart attack? Stroke?" asked Winston.

"Murder. On the high school track early this morning."

Winston seemed genuinely shocked. "Good heavens! Does Harold know?"

"Yes, he does," said Myrtle. "I assume he'll be here shortly, though I wouldn't blame him if he chose to skip this gathering."

Winston looked around the gymnasium. "Two of our class-mates murdered within days of each other. This is most disturb-ing."

Myrtle noticed Gladys appeared to be trying to get every-one's attention. Either that, or she was having some sort of coughing attack. She was constantly clearing her throat. Gladys looked at Myrtle for help. Retired schoolteacher Myrtle imme-diately clapped her hands and said, "Everyone! Gladys wants to speak."

There was immediate silence. "Thank you," said Gladys, now looking shy with the attention on her. "Let's get started."

Myrtle noticed Gladys somehow hadn't gotten enough chairs out. One would think there would be more than ex-pected, just in case. Especially since she should have thought Evie and Harold would be in attendance. Miles was an extra at-tendee, but even if he hadn't been there, there wouldn't have been enough seats.

This had the effect of putting Miles in an agony of em-barrassment for crashing the memorial service. "I'll stand in the back," he whispered to Myrtle. He looked like a child who hadn't found a seat during musical chairs.

"Nonsense," said Myrtle. "Gladys, there aren't enough chairs. Which classroom did you acquire these from?"

Gladys was immediately flustered. "Oh, dear. I'm so sorry."

"I'll get one," said Frank, heading toward a stack of chairs in the corner that Myrtle hadn't spotted.

"Maybe get a couple," said Myrtle. "Just in case."

Frank returned with the chairs, placing them next to the others in a circle. It looked more like a group therapy setup than a memorial service to Myrtle. As they settled into their seats, Harold arrived, looking pale and drawn, his previously distinguished appearance now marked by grief.

"Thank you all for coming," began Gladys. "We're here to remember our dear friend Belinda Holloway, whose life was tragically cut short."

Harold cleared his throat. "If I may," he said, his voice strained. "My wife Evie was also murdered this morning. I think it's appropriate that we remember her as well."

A murmur ran through the small group. Millie's face went slack with shock, and Winston shook his head sadly. Gladys looked momentarily flustered, but recovered quickly.

"Of course, Harold. How terrible. We'll certainly include Evie in our memorial." She looked around the circle. "Would anyone like to start by sharing a memory of either Belinda or Evie?"

There was an uncomfortable silence. Myrtle suspected none of them had been close to either woman, despite what Gladys had claimed about her friendship with Belinda.

Finally, Winston spoke up. "Belinda had a remarkable zest for life," he said. "Even back in high school, she was always planning something, organizing events, making things happen. I admired her energy and enthusiasm."

Frank nodded. "She was certainly driven. Knew what she wanted and went after it."

Myrtle thought she detected a hint of bitterness in Frank's tone.

"And Evie," said Gladys, turning to Harold, "was always so supportive of you, Harold. Such a devoted wife."

Harold nodded solemnly. "Fifty-eight years," he said softly. "We were married fifty-eight years."

Miles glanced at Myrtle, perhaps wondering if she was going to say something. Myrtle remained silent, preferring to observe the dynamics of the group.

"I'd like to say something about Belinda," said Millie suddenly. Everyone turned to look at her. "Belinda was ambitious, and she was smart. She knew how to get what she wanted, even if it meant stepping on others to get it."

The bluntness of Millie's statement hung in the air. Frank coughed awkwardly.

"Well, ambition isn't necessarily a bad thing," said Winston diplomatically.

"It is when it's at the expense of others," said Millie. Her tone was sharp, her eyes hard.

"I think what Millie means," said Myrtle, "is that Belinda was complex, like all of us. She had her strengths and her flaws."

Millie looked at Myrtle with surprise, perhaps not expecting her to come to her defense—or at least soften her criticism.

Gladys looked uncomfortable. "Would anyone like some refreshments before we continue? We have some lovely food, including a unique Jell-O salad that Myrtle brought."

Miles suppressed a smile.

Harold moved away from the circle and toward the middle of the gym, but no one was in any hurry to follow him, perhaps because they weren't sure what to say. Myrtle had decided long ago that there was *nothing* good to say in these circumstances, but it was worse ignoring the situation altogether. She walked toward him, with Miles following at a discreet distance.

Harold looked at her with tired eyes. "I still can't believe it, Myrtle."

"No. You'd been together for so long. It was quite nice of you to make the service, considering the horrid day you've had."

Harold shrugged. "I was going insane stuck in that hotel room. It's better to be here." He glowered around the room. "Even if one of these people is a killer."

"Have the police made any progress? That Shaw person—did he provide any information?" asked Myrtle.

Harold frowned. "He seemed more interested in my relationship with Belinda than in finding out who killed my wife."

"That's rather bizarre, isn't it? What did he want to know about Belinda?"

"I don't know. The questions were ridiculous, really."

Myrtle nodded thoughtfully. "Shaw seems to have some strange notions."

"Like suspecting you," said Harold with a small smile.

"Yes, well, Lieutenant Shaw isn't exactly Hercule Poirot," said Myrtle.

"Hardly," agreed Harold. "Although I could picture him with a big mustache." He looked around him, an exhausted expression on his face. "Even though I wanted to get out, I don't think I realized how exhausting this would be."

"It's understandable if you'd like to leave early," said Myrtle. "No one would think less of you."

Harold nodded. "I might. But first, I'd like to speak about Evie. Make sure she's properly remembered. I wasn't sure what to say before, but I think I have more of an inkling now."

They joined the others at the refreshment table, where Gladys was trying to coax people into trying Myrtle's Jell-O salad.

"It's very creative," Gladys was saying, stirring the still-liquefied concoction with a spoon.

"I don't think it quite set," admitted Myrtle. "There might have been too much fruit cocktail syrup."

"What are these red things?" asked Frank, peering into the bowl.

"Maraschino cherries, of course," said Myrtle. "Don't tell me you've never had Jell-O salad before."

"Not quite like this," said Frank, taking a small spoonful.

Harold murmured to Gladys a moment. As the group settled back into their chairs with various refreshments, Gladys called the group back to order, more successfully this time. "Harold would like to say a few words about Evie," she announced.

Harold stood slowly, using his cane for support. "Evie was the best person I've ever known," he began, his voice thick with emotion. "She was kind, patient, and far more understanding than I deserved. We met in high school, but it wasn't until after I finished medical school that we got married. She waited for me all those years."

Myrtle watched the faces of the others as Harold spoke. Millie looked uncomfortable, staring down at her hands. Frank was listening intently, his expression somber. Winston seemed genuinely moved, dabbing at his eyes with a handkerchief.

"Evie was a wonderful teacher," continued Harold. "She loved her students and poured her heart into her work. She was also a devoted mother to our children and grandmother to our grandchildren. I don't know how I'll go on without her."

Harold's voice broke on the last words, and he sat down, overcome with emotion. Millie, surprising everyone, reached over and patted his hand awkwardly.

Harold stood up, using his cane to assist in the process. "I think I need to go," he said. "This has been difficult."

"Of course, Harold," said Gladys sympathetically. "Do you need a ride back to the hotel?"

"No, thank you. I'll be able to drive back."

Chapter Nineteen

After Harold left, the atmosphere in the gymnasium lightened slightly. Myrtle noticed Frank watching Miles and her. When their eyes met, he approached them.

"Do you two have plans after this?" he asked. "I was thinking we might talk more about what's happened. Maybe over coffee or something?"

Myrtle glanced at Miles, who gave a subtle nod. "That sounds fine," she said. "Where would you like to meet?"

"How about Bo's Diner?" suggested Frank. "In about thirty minutes?"

"That will be perfect," said Myrtle. "Miles and I will meet you there."

As Frank walked away, Miles leaned close to Myrtle. "I'm wondering if you and I are thinking the same thing?"

"That Frank is either worried about being a suspect or has information he wants to share?" said Myrtle. "Yes."

"Or maybe he wants to pump us for information about the investigation," added Miles.

"Either way," said Myrtle, "it should be an enlightening conversation."

Miles nodded. "Especially now that there's been another murder."

Myrtle glanced over at Millie, who was speaking with Winston. "I'm still curious about Millie's connection to all this. She was quite harsh in her eulogy. If that was a eulogy at all, which is highly debatable."

"She certainly was. It was almost as if she couldn't contain her venom, even though Belinda isn't here to hear it. Then there's the fact that Harold mentioned Millie had arranged to meet Evie for a walk this morning," said Miles.

"Yes, that is quite curious," agreed Myrtle. "But let's focus on Frank for now. We can try to speak with Millie another time."

As they prepared to leave, Gladys approached them. "Myrtle, would you like to take your Jell-O salad home? We didn't quite finish it."

Myrtle looked over at the table where her creation sat, still in its liquid state, with only a small amount missing. "No, thank you, Gladys. Please feel free to enjoy it yourself. I put it in a disposable container so it wouldn't have to be returned to me."

Gladys looked briefly panicked, then recovered. "How thoughtful of you."

Miles chuckled quietly as they left the gymnasium.

"What's so funny?" asked Myrtle.

"Nothing," said Miles. "Just appreciating your generosity in sharing your Jell-O salad with Gladys."

"It was the least I could do," said Myrtle.

They arrived at Bo's Diner before Frank. Myrtle selected a booth near the back, away from the other diners. She wanted privacy for their conversation.

"What's our strategy?" asked Miles as they settled into the vinyl seats.

"Let's see what Frank has to say first," said Myrtle. "I suspect he's more likely to talk if we listen instead of our jumping right in with questions."

Miles nodded. "And if he doesn't volunteer anything?"

"Then we'll have to be more direct," said Myrtle. "But subtly, of course."

Frank arrived a few minutes later, looking around the diner before spotting them. He slid into the booth across from Myrtle and Miles.

"Thanks for meeting me," he said, placing his hands on the table. Myrtle noticed they were trembling slightly.

"Happy to," said Myrtle. "It was a nice service, considering the circumstances."

Frank nodded. "As nice as those things can be, I guess. But Evie? This is like a nightmare."

"It is concerning," said Myrtle.

"And both deaths at the high school," offered Miles.

Frank frowned. "I wonder if the cops are really thinking through their suspects. I haven't been impressed with what I've seen so far. I mean, your son has been great, Myrtle, really great."

"Has he?" asked Myrtle dryly.

"Well, sure. It's just Shaw and those other state cops. I don't think they're looking at this stuff the right way up. Maybe it's some deranged high school kid, you know?"

"Deranged high-schooler?" Myrtle tilted her head to one side.

"Yeah. Hey, that's not any more surprising than deranged octogenarians. Why couldn't it be a kid?"

The waitress came, blessedly sparing Myrtle from replying. Despite the offerings at the memorial service, no one had really eaten much. Myrtle ordered a pimento cheese chili dog with fries, which made Miles look rather green at the gills. Frank ordered a triple-decker burger with chili fries. Miles decided on the garden salad, which made Myrtle roll her eyes.

Frank looked as if he might continue his train of thought on the subject of suspects. "On the other hand, I'm not saying it *couldn't* be somebody from our group. What about Harold?"

Myrtle was game to consider any suspect who wasn't a homicidal teen at this point. "What makes you think Harold might have killed Belinda and Evie?"

"Well, think about it. We know Harold and Belinda had history together."

Miles looked as if he might have missed something. "History? Harold and Belinda were having an affair?"

"No, no. Well, not as far as I know, anyway. I mean, they had history back in high school."

Miles said slowly, "Does what happened in high school even matter anymore?"

"Maybe to some people it does. Maybe folks aren't happy with the way their lives turned out, and they blame it all on their high school years."

Myrtle said, "I'm trying to figure out your position on this. You're saying Evie was upset about Belinda dating Harold in high school and killed Belinda? Then Harold killed Evie? His wife?" Her head was pounding as it attempted to follow Frank's derailed train of thought.

"Harold seemed genuinely distraught about Evie's death," said Miles.

"Anyone can put on an act," insisted Frank. "And didn't you see how uncomfortable he was at the service? Something was off."

"The fact he was grieving?" asked Myrtle archly. Frank looked a bit deflated and Myrtle said, "Okay, I'll play along a bit. Harold seemed upset to me during that scavenger hunt at the reunion. Distressed. He was speaking with Belinda and something definitely seemed wrong."

"See? And now she's dead." Frank was nodding his head eagerly.

Miles said slowly, "But why would Harold kill Belinda? I don't get it."

Frank lowered his voice, even though there was no way anyone in the busy diner would overhear them. "Maybe she threatened him somehow. Belinda was the sort who knew everybody's business and stored tidbits away that might be useful later."

Their food arrived, and they were quiet for a few moments as they took bites and waited for the waitress to move away. Frank continued, "Harold's been a big name in the area for a while. Plus, he has tons of money. Maybe he has something he wants to keep quiet."

Myrtle said, "Last time, you said you thought Gladys might have had it in for Belinda. You said Gladys thought she and Belinda were these great friends when they really weren't."

"Yeah, that's what Belinda told me." Frank shrugged. "I mean, who knows? Can we see Gladys killing Evie, though? I could totally see Gladys getting upset with Belinda and losing it, but murdering Evie feels like a stretch."

"Unless Evie knew something," said Miles. He seemed surprised that he'd spoken and quickly returned to his salad.

"True," said Frank.

Myrtle said, "What about Millie?"

Frank frowned. "What about Millie?"

"Do you think Millie could be responsible for these deaths?"

Frank snorted. "Nerdy Millie Thatcher? Scavenger hunt winner? What makes you think she would do something like that. She's the kind of person who wouldn't jaywalk even if there wasn't a car in sight."

Myrtle said, "Harold mentioned Millie arranged to meet up with Evie this morning to exercise."

Frank's eyebrows drew down. "No way. Was she there? When you found Evie?"

"No. She wasn't anywhere around."

Frank looked thoughtful. "That's really weird, especially since Millie and Evie were never friends. And since when does Millie exercise? She's not exactly the athletic type."

"Perhaps she's changed?" suggested Miles.

"Not that much," said Frank. He took a sip of his coffee. "I still think Harold is more likely. He had connections to both victims."

"So did you," pointed out Myrtle.

Frank nearly choked on his coffee. "What?"

"I understand you were arguing with Belinda during the scavenger hunt. Apparently, you were blaming Belinda for your grandson's death."

Frank's face flushed with anger. "That was private."

"Apparently, you weren't keeping your voice down. And I'm not accusing you; I'm simply pointing out that several people have potential motives," said Myrtle.

Frank set his coffee cup down with a thud on the table. "I didn't kill anyone. Yes, I was seriously irritated with Belinda. She invested in a pain management clinic that got my grandson hooked on pills. He died because of those people and their lax prescription practices. But I wouldn't kill her over it."

"I believe you," said Myrtle, though she wasn't entirely sure she did. "I'm just trying to understand what happened."

Frank seemed to deflate slightly. "I know. I'm sorry for getting defensive. But Tyler's death is still a raw wound, though, you know? The two of us used to always be a pair on the weekends—he was my fishing buddy." He swallowed hard, then seemed to get control of himself again. He angrily said, "Seeing Belinda at the reunion, acting like she hadn't a care in the world? It made me see red."

"That's only natural, considering Belinda had ties to the clinic," said Myrtle. She paused. "I'm surprised Belinda invested in a clinic in a different town. I know she lived in Atlanta."

"She still returned to Bradley from time to time to see her sister, apparently. And, I guess, to oversee the clinic."

Myrtle said, "Oh, that's right. I remember Winston saying Belinda's sister resided somewhere here."

Frank looked down at his coffee, then back up at Myrtle. "There's something else you should know. About Gladys."

"What about her?"

"She's broke," said Frank bluntly. "Has been for years. She's living on a tiny pension and barely making ends meet. But she was telling everyone that Belinda was going to leave her something in her will. Like a windfall."

"And was she?" asked Miles.

Frank shook his head. "No way. I don't think Gladys was getting a dime. It was all just wishful thinking on her part." He leaned forward again. "But here's the thing. Gladys was desperate. She needs money for dental work, home repairs, all sorts of things. What if she killed Belinda in a moment of rage? And what if Evie saw her do it, like we were saying before? Evie was a witness?"

"Why would Evie wait days to confront Gladys, if she saw her kill Belinda?" asked Miles.

Frank frowned. "I don't know. Maybe she wasn't sure what she saw. Maybe she was afraid."

"Or maybe someone else entirely is responsible," suggested Myrtle. "Someone with connections to both Belinda and Evie."

"Like who?" asked Frank.

Myrtle sipped her coffee. "That's what I'm trying to figure out."

Frank looked uncomfortable for a moment, fidgeting with his coffee cup.

"Is there something else, Frank?" asked Myrtle.

"Yeah. I got a call from Belinda's attorney yesterday. She left me a lot of money in her will."

"*Did* she? That's rather remarkable, isn't it?" asked Myrtle.

"Yeah," said Frank again. "The lawyer said it was listed as reparations. My daughter got money, too. The lawyer said it was 'partial restitution for the pain clinic's role in Tyler's death.'"

Myrtle said, "What did you make of that?"

Frank's voice was rough. "It was typical that Belinda thought money would make everything all right. I lost my grandson. But I guess it was the best she could do. Then, I got to thinking about it. The lawyer wouldn't give me information about anything else in the will, but I called Millie."

Myrtle raised an eyebrow. "You were wondering if Belinda might have left her something, as well?"

"Right. I knew there was bad blood between Millie and Belinda from all the way back to high school. I thought maybe Belinda had tried to make it right. Sure enough, Millie said she'd gotten a call from the lawyer, too. A bequest, labeled as reparations." Frank looked at his watch. "I should get going. I have some stuff I need to take care of. And I bet the cops are going to want to interview everybody again now that Evie is dead."

"Of course," said Myrtle. "Thanks for having breakfast with us."

As Frank was leaving, he turned back. "Be careful, Myrtle. You too, Miles. Someone is killing off our classmates. You wouldn't want to be next."

Chapter Twenty

After Frank left, Miles looked at Myrtle. "That was rather ominous."

"Indeed," said Myrtle. "Though I'm not sure if he was warning us or threatening us."

"What did you make of Frank's theories?" asked Miles.

Myrtle considered for a moment. "He raised interesting points about Harold and about Gladys's financial troubles. But he seemed eager to point fingers away from himself, didn't he?"

"He did get quite defensive when you mentioned his argument with Belinda," noted Miles.

"Very," agreed Myrtle. "And yet he was quick to share theories about the others."

"So what's next?" asked Miles.

Myrtle sighed. "I think we need to speak with Millie. Find out if she really did arrange to meet Evie this morning. And if so, why she didn't show up."

"And if Millie didn't make those plans to meet up at the track, that would suggest Harold was lying," said Miles.

"Exactly," said Myrtle. "Someone is lying. And I'd very much like to know who."

Miles pushed his glasses up his nose and looked anxiously around the diner. "Do you think we're in danger? Like Frank suggested?"

"Perhaps," admitted Myrtle. "But I don't intend to let that stop me from finding the truth."

Miles gave her a wry look. "I didn't think it would."

They finished their coffees, and Miles paid the bill. As they were getting in the car, Myrtle paused.

"One more thing," she said. "I'd like to find out more about Harold, especially his reputation at work. If Belinda was blackmailing him over it, that could be a strong motive."

"How do we do that?" asked Miles.

Myrtle smiled. "I think it's time we paid a visit to Greener Pastures Retirement Home. If anyone would know about old medical scandals, it would be the residents there."

"Red would be delighted to know you're going there. Perhaps he'll think it's a reconnaissance mission."

"We'll just have to make sure he doesn't find out," said Myrtle, putting on her seatbelt.

Miles shook his head, looking as though his garden salad wasn't sitting well in his stomach. "I have a feeling this isn't going to end well."

"Nonsense," said Myrtle briskly. "It's going to end with us solving two murders. What could be better than that?"

"Not being involved in the investigation of two murders in the first place?" suggested Miles.

"Where's your sense of adventure, Miles?" chided Myrtle. "Besides, we're already involved. We might as well see it through to the end."

Miles nodded with resignation. "I suppose you're right."

"Naturally," said Myrtle.

They made the drive over to Greener Pastures. The retirement home had been trying, somewhat unsuccessfully, to rebrand itself by calling themselves a retirement "village." However, it didn't remotely resemble a village in Myrtle's mind. It looked like a place that was trying hard to appear more upscale than it actually was. But it was all skin-level: new coats of paint, a new sign with brick pillars and ironwork, and some new carpeting. Yet the food was horrendous and the resident care was spotty.

Miles, however, had never considered it such a terrible place. This was made clear once again when they walked inside and there was a sign calling attention to a chess competition taking place the next day. "Sounds like chess is big here."

"Is it?" asked Myrtle. "I wouldn't have thought so. The only thing that seems to be big here is the medication cart. It's practically the size of a school bus."

Miles gave her a look. "Now, now. You really have a grudge against this place."

"Red's the one who gave me the grudge." Myrtle started setting off toward one of the day rooms.

"Do you know where we're going?" asked Miles. "Do you have specific people you want to speak with?"

But Myrtle wasn't listening. She appeared to be distracted by the earsplitting volume level of a television inside one of the residents' rooms. "Are they trying to communicate with the dead?"

"They must be hard of hearing," said Miles.

"That's putting it lightly."

Miles decided to ask his question again. "Do you have a game plan for finding out information about Harold's medical career?"

Myrtle shook her head and said coolly, "Not necessary. Everyone here is eager to see a new face and happy to talk. I'm sure we'll find out all sorts of information without even trying."

But at first, it didn't seem to be that way at all. They were stuck speaking with an old woman who wanted to tell them, in great detail, about the different pets she'd owned in her lifetime. It was quite impossible to get away until Miles suddenly had a coughing fit and Myrtle dragged him off to locate a water fountain.

She was surprised to see he was still coughing when they rounded the corner. "I thought you were putting that cough on as a front to get us away from that woman."

Miles shook his head, still hacking and quite red in the face. Finally, the coughing subsided after he had a few sips from the water fountain. Speaking was still beyond him, though, so Myrtle launched into her own monologue. Thankfully, not about a lifetime of pets. "Perhaps a more targeted approach to our information gathering *is* in order. I'd forgotten how chatty some inmates here can be."

"Residents," Miles wheezed out.

"They're more like inmates, really, aren't they? Anyway, let's continue on our way to the day room. We just ran into a roadblock with that Chatty Kathy over there. I'll be more cautious next time."

Miles nodded mutely, and they set off for the day room. However, they were delayed by a tremendous traffic jam involving a couple of old men on walkers and several wheelchairs inhabited by residents who didn't want to try to pass them.

On the way, they passed a health room, a chapel, and the dining hall. "Avoid the cafeteria at all costs," advised Myrtle. "Apparently, the food has gotten even more atrocious."

Miles cast a wistful look at it. "I had an excellent carrot cake there once."

"Once, Miles. That was clearly an anomaly. Perhaps one of the staff members brought in a birthday cake."

Finally, they reached one of the day rooms. There were groups of residents playing what looked like mahjong, a group watching a reality show of some kind, and, to Myrtle's dismay, a table with Winston and a puzzle. She grabbed Miles and was about to urge them to make their escape when he spotted them and walked over.

"My dear Myrtle," he said, reaching for her hand, which she snatched away quickly before he could bestow a courtly kiss on it. "And Melrose."

"Miles," said Miles, rather stiffly this time, as if he suspected Winston was getting his name wrong on purpose.

"Ah, of course. Sorry about that, my friend. The old brain cells aren't quite as lively as they used to be."

Miles looked over at the puzzle. "You're making good headway on the jigsaw, though."

"Come and take a look. Maybe you and Myrtle can lend me a hand."

They joined him at the table, which seated four. "Notre Dame," said Myrtle. She reached out, plucked up a puzzle piece, and fit it immediately into a spot.

Miles, not to be outdone, did the same.

Winston chuckled. "What perceptive guests I have today. Thanks for coming to see me."

Myrtle was now quite irritated. She was sure Winston had nothing useful to offer, he was an incorrigible flirt, and her trip to the retirement home had been hijacked.

Miles sensed her annoyance and, in good sidekick fashion, stepped in for Myrtle. "We were hoping we'd run into you, but we were here on a bit of a mission. Maybe you can help us with it."

"Intriguing! I would love being deputized." He leaned in closer. "Are you embroiled in investigating the horrid crimes? For the newspaper, perhaps?"

Myrtle nodded. Her mind was still trying to form excuses to remove them from Winston's vicinity in order to speak with someone actually useful.

"I'm in!" said Winston delightedly. "What would you like to know? I'm a veritable font of information."

Since Myrtle was clearly still unengaged, Miles said, "We were wondering if you knew much about Frank Lawson. He's not a resident at Greener Pastures, of course, but maybe you have a bit of information on him. Especially pertaining to his grandson."

Now Myrtle's irritation found a new target—in Miles. That wasn't their mission at all. They were trying to learn about

Harold's career and if there had been any missteps. It was all very annoying that Miles was going off the rails.

Winston said, "Oh yes, good old Frank. He's not had the easiest time of it, has he?"

"Hasn't he?" asked Miles.

"Sadly, no. His poor grandson, you know. He was so very fond of the lad. Fishing and whatnot." Winston looked rather vague about the fishing. It was clearly not his preferred sport. Myrtle, looking at his preppy attire, guessed he might be more of a cricket fan.

Myrtle said, "I'm surprised you're friendly with Frank. I don't recall the two of you being friends in high school."

"No, no, Frank was too much of an athlete, wasn't he? Always in the gym or lifting weights or whatever those folks do. But now, you see, he's over here at the Village."

Winston had obviously taken the bait and switched over to calling Greener Pastures the Village. "But he's not a resident here," said Myrtle. "At least, he claimed not to be." He'd told them he lived out on the old rural route highway, like Wanda.

"No, he lives elsewhere. But he does lead a seniors' exercise program here on Tuesdays and Thursdays. Frank worked hard to persuade me to come and kudos to him for that. I wouldn't have darkened the door of the class if he hadn't been so very encouraging. It's been a surprisingly rewarding experience."

Myrtle had no desire to hear about Winston's workout. "But about Frank's grandson."

"Yes, yes. A tragic thing, really. I could tell something was weighing on the man, you know. He was so very dedicated to the exercise program until his grandson's problems started. Such a shame what happened to that boy."

Miles watched as Myrtle narrowed her eyes impatiently at Winston. He said, "It was drugs, wasn't it?"

"That's absolutely correct, Miles, yes. Frank lent Tyler, that's his grandson, five thousand dollars for a used car." Winston shook his head sorrowfully. "The boy spent it on drugs. Then Frank drained his retirement savings to pay for Tyler's rehab. A terrible matter. Then there was the impact on the family dynamics."

"How were those impacts?" asked Myrtle.

"Atrocious. Frank's daughter (that's Tyler's mother, you see), blamed Frank for funding his drug problem."

Miles said slowly, "But Frank thought he was helping Tyler by buying him a car."

"Yes, but Frank's daughter apparently felt the need to blame someone, and Frank was a convenient target. The whole thing started when Tyler, an athlete like his grandfather, was prescribed opioids after a sports injury of some kind. He went to this pain management center, which continued prescribing the drugs even after Tyler's injury should have been healed." Winston peered at a puzzle piece, crowing when it fit into one of the church spires.

Myrtle said, "And Tyler ended up dying from a drug overdose, I understand."

"Unfortunately. The rehab didn't seem to take, and he took to cheaper street drugs after the clinic finally refused further prescriptions."

Miles said carefully, "Was there some sort of connection between the clinic and Belinda?"

"Now that you mention it, yes. Gracious. I'd totally forgotten that. Belinda was a major investor in the pain management clinic. Frank mentioned that he'd called Belinda and given her a piece of his mind. But Belinda told him she was merely a hands-off investor and not someone involved in it on a day-to-day basis."

"Was that true?" asked Myrtle.

Winston beamed at her. "Astute as always! Your mind has always been a wonder to me. No, it wasn't true at all. Frank found out Belinda had ignored complaints about over-prescribing. In fact, Belinda used her influence as an investor to block efforts to implement stricter protocols at the clinic."

Miles frowned. "That's awful."

"Isn't it?" asked Winston. "Apparently, Belinda and the other investors were making money hand-over-fist and didn't want a thing changed. She became a wealthy woman, not that I think she was suffering financially even before the clinic. Belinda did well with her real estate business." Then Winston gave a smile. "Then everything fell down around her."

"Lawsuits," said Myrtle.

Winston clapped his hands together. "Brilliant again! Yes, there was a class-action lawsuit against the clinic. Belinda, because of her efforts blocking changes, bore significant financial responsibility."

"So she was punished, in a sense. She lost her money," said Myrtle.

Winston shook his head sadly. "Many things in life aren't fair. She did lose some money. But she still had plenty of money somewhere. Offshore? Invested in real estate? At any rate, the suit didn't eliminate her wealth."

"But in Frank's mind, she received some retribution for her actions, I'd imagine," said Myrtle.

Winston raised his eyebrows. "But was it enough to satisfy Frank? That's the question, isn't it?"

Before Myrtle could respond, a piercing voice cut through the dayroom. "Bingo in five minutes! Everyone to the activity room for bingo."

The effect was immediate. Residents who'd, moments earlier, appeared to be napping suddenly leaped into action. Wheelchairs were turned, walkers were grabbed, and a slow but determined migration began.

Chapter Twenty-One

"Gracious," said Winston. "It's bingo day. My apologies, but I'm afraid I must participate. They do have marvelous prizes."

"Prizes?" Miles appeared curious, despite himself.

"Oh, yes. Last week, I won a lovely tin of butter cookies. At least, I believed it to be a cookie container. It ended up being a sewing kit. You're welcome to join us. The more, the merrier."

Myrtle had no intention of playing bingo when they were supposed to be gathering information about Harold Blackwood. But before she could protest, a small, wiry woman with tightly permed white hair swooped down on them.

"Winston! There you are. And you've brought friends." She beamed at Myrtle and Miles. "I'm Doris, the activities director. You simply must join us for bingo."

"Actually—" Myrtle began.

"No, no, I insist!" said Doris, taking Myrtle's arm with surprising strength. "We love having visitors participate. It brightens everyone's day."

Miles and Myrtle were swept along with the crowd. The activity room was already filling with residents, many of whom were eyeing Myrtle and Miles with undisguised curiosity.

"Newcomers," one elderly woman stage-whispered to her neighbor. "They don't look happy to be here."

"Probably scouting the place out," the neighbor replied just as loudly.

Myrtle bristled. "I'll have you know I'm perfectly capable of living independently."

This only seemed to confirm their suspicions. "That's what Mildred said right before she moved in," the first woman nodded sagely.

Before Myrtle could further protest, they were seated at a table with Winston and two other residents. Doris handed them each a bingo card and a handful of markers.

"The winner of each round gets to choose from our prize basket," she announced, pointing to a wicker basket filled with what appeared to be an assortment of travel-sized toiletries, puzzle books, and socks.

Miles leaned over to Myrtle. "Perhaps we should just play one round to be polite, then try to find someone who might know about Harold?"

"This is a complete waste of time," Myrtle muttered, but she arranged her markers on the card, nonetheless.

"B-7!" called Doris with an enthusiasm that seemed excessive for the occasion.

Winston dabbed his card with gusto. "Oh, I feel lucky today!"

"I-22!"

The woman across from Myrtle, who had yet to introduce herself, suddenly leaned forward. "Are you two married?" she asked bluntly.

"No," said Myrtle and Miles in unison.

"Hmm." The woman narrowed her eyes. "Roommates then?"

"Neighbors," said Miles.

"G-59!"

"Special friends," the woman said with a knowing nod.

Myrtle glared at her. "Do you mind? I'm trying to concentrate on my bingo card."

The woman sniffed. "Well, excuse me for making conversation. I've been married three times myself. Outlived all of them."

"How fortunate for them," Myrtle said under her breath.

"O-67!"

"BINGO!" shouted Winston, waving his card triumphantly. Doris hurried over to verify his win, then presented him with the prize basket.

"Winston, you lucky dog." said the man to Miles's right, speaking for the first time. He was balding with liver spots dotting his scalp, and he wore thick glasses that magnified his eyes to an alarming degree. "That's three weeks in a row."

"The system, Harold," Winston tapped his temple. "I've developed a system for winning bingo."

Myrtle had enough bingo talk. She broke in. "I'm Myrtle, and this is Miles. We're trying to find out information about Dr. Harold Blackwood. He's a surgeon. Would you happen to know anything about him?"

Winkler shook his head. "Doctors? No, can't say I do. My doctor's a young fella, barely looks old enough to drive."

The three-times-widowed woman suddenly perked up. "The surgeon? Of course. He removed my gallbladder back in '85. Or was it '86? No matter. Handsome man. Very steady hands."

"You know him?" Myrtle leaned forward eagerly.

"Know him? I practically proposed to him after he took out that gallbladder. Would have too, if I hadn't been married to my Henry at the time."

"And what did you think of him? Professionally, I mean."

The woman waved a hand dismissively. "Oh, he was fine. No complaints. Well, except for that business with the Jensen boy."

Myrtle's eyes widened. "What business?"

"B-12!" Doris called out, and the woman's attention snapped back to her bingo card.

"I've got that one," she muttered, placing a marker.

"What about the Jensen boy?" Myrtle persisted.

"What? Oh, that. It was nothing really. Just some talk about a surgery gone wrong," said the woman carelessly.

"N-43!"

"Please," Myrtle said, "could you tell me more about—"

"BINGO!" shrieked the woman suddenly, throwing her arms up in victory. "I told Henry I'd win today. He came to me in a dream last night. Said, 'Mabel, you're due for a win.' And here it is!"

As Mabel went to claim her prize, Myrtle turned to Miles in frustration. "This is hopeless. We need to find someone who can give us actual information, not just gossip and hearsay."

"Perhaps we could ask at the nurses' station?" suggested Miles. "They might know of former hospital employees who live here."

But before they could make their escape, Winston returned with his prize—a small bottle of hand sanitizer—which he promptly presented to Miles.

"For you, my friend," he said magnanimously. "I noticed you seem to appreciate cleanliness."

Miles accepted the gift with genuine gratitude. "Thank you, Winston. That's very thoughtful."

"Now," said Winston, "shall we try for another round? I'm feeling particularly fortunate today."

"Actually," said Myrtle, rising from her seat, "Miles and I need to—"

"Oh, look!" interrupted Doris, pointing to the doorway. "It's time for our special entertainment."

A middle-aged man wearing an ill-fitting cowboy outfit complete with boots and hat strode into the room carrying a guitar. "Howdy, partners," he called out. "Who's ready for some country classics?"

The room erupted in cheers.

"Please kill me now," Myrtle muttered to Miles.

The cowboy launched into an off-key rendition of a Hank Williams song, encouraging everyone to clap along. Winston was tapping his foot enthusiastically and mouthing the words.

"We need to get out of here," Myrtle said firmly.

Miles nodded, and they began making their way toward the door, only to find their path blocked by a line of residents in wheelchairs who had formed an impromptu chorus line, rolling back and forth in time to the music.

"Excuse me," Myrtle said, trying to squeeze past. "Pardon me."

"You folks leaving already?" called the cowboy between verses. "I'm just getting warmed up. This next one's for all the lovebirds out there—including our special visitors!"

He pointed directly at Myrtle and Miles, and the entire room turned to stare at them.

"Oh, for heaven's sake," Myrtle grumbled. "We are not love-birds."

"Don't be shy now," the cowboy grinned. "This one's called 'Forever Young at Heart,' and I wrote it myself."

"Remarkable," said Miles weakly.

The cowboy launched into what appeared to be an inter-minable ballad about aging sweethearts, with many references to rocking chairs, sunset years, and holding hands through eter-nity.

Two verses in, Myrtle had had enough. She motioned to Miles, who followed her out of the room. She said, "We learned absolutely nothing useful about Harold Blackwood, and I wasn't about to sit through that dreadful man's entire reper-toire."

As they approached the main entrance, they spotted a famil-iar figure heading their way. It was Winston Rouse, slightly out of breath.

"There you are," he called. "I thought I might have missed you."

Myrtle stifled a groan. "Winston. How persistent of you."

"I realized I might help with your inquiries about Dr. Blackwood," he said. "I couldn't help but overhear you at the bingo table. You see, my roommate for a brief time was an orderly at the hospital where Harold worked."

"Is he here now?" asked Myrtle, suddenly interested.

"No, I'm afraid he's passed on. Pancreatic cancer, poor fellow. But he did mention something once about Dr. Blackwood having a bit of trouble with alcohol back in the day. Said he came in smelling of bourbon one night when he was on call."

"Did that affect his work?" Miles asked.

Winston shrugged. "Roger—that was my roommate—never said specifically. Just that it was hushed up rather quickly. The hospital administration was quite protective of their star surgeon."

It wasn't much, but it was something. "Thank you, Winston," Myrtle said. "That's actually helpful."

Winston beamed. "Always glad to be of service, my dear Myrtle." He took her hand before she could stop him and planted a kiss on it. "Perhaps next time you visit, you'll stay for the full bingo session? I find the competition quite invigorating."

"Perhaps," said Myrtle noncommittally, withdrawing her hand and wiping it surreptitiously on her slacks.

"And you too, Maurice."

"Miles," corrected Miles with a sigh.

"Yes, of course. My apologies." Winston tapped his temple again. "The old memory isn't what it used to be. Good day to you both."

"That man is insufferable," Myrtle muttered as they walked to Miles's car. "And the entire visit was a waste of time. We barely learned anything useful about Harold."

"We did learn he might have had some issues with alcohol," Miles pointed out. "And if he was operating while impaired, that could certainly be something Belinda might have known about. And that woman mentioned something about a Jensen boy."

"True," Myrtle conceded. "But we need more than just vague rumors. We need facts."

"What next, then?" asked Miles as they settled into the car.

"I need to write up my article for the newspaper," said Myrtle. "I texted Sloan earlier and he'll be expecting it. And then tomorrow, I think we should pay a visit to Gladys. She seems to be at the center of a lot of this, between her financial troubles and her fantasy friendship with Belinda."

Miles nodded. "I'll drop you at home, then."

"Thank goodness," said Myrtle. "I need to wash my hands with real soap after that visit. And possibly my ears as well, after that cowboy's caterwauling."

Miles chuckled as he pulled away from Greener Pastures. "It wasn't that harrowing."

"It was worse," insisted Myrtle. "And if Red ever tries to entomb me in that place, I'll haunt him relentlessly for eternity."

"I'd expect nothing less," said Miles.

Chapter Twenty-Two

Back at her house, Myrtle settled at her computer to write her article for the Bradley Bugle. The story of Evie's murder would be front-page news, and Myrtle was determined to do it justice while also dropping subtle hints about potential connections to Belinda's death.

She had just finished her first draft when her phone rang. It was Sloan.

"Miss Myrtle," he said, his voice tight with anxiety. "About that article on the second murder. Please tell me you're nearly done. The press is waiting."

"I'm sending it now, Sloan," she said, hitting the send button. "It's a comprehensive piece that links both murders, with background on the victims and potential motives."

"Comprehensive?" Sloan's voice rose an octave. "I was thinking more of a brief announcement. Red already called to remind me that releasing too many details might compromise his investigation."

"Nonsense," said Myrtle. "The people of Bradley deserve thorough reporting. My article simply presents the facts."

"Your version of the facts," Sloan muttered, then quickly added, "which are always impeccably researched, of course."

"Of course," said Myrtle dryly.

"It's just that Red specifically mentioned—"

"As far as I'm aware, Red is not the editor of the Bradley Bugle," Myrtle interrupted. "You are. And a fine editor would stand by his crime reporter."

There was a pause, and Myrtle could practically hear Sloan's internal struggle.

"Have I mentioned how much everyone enjoyed your helpful hints column last week?" he said finally. "Mrs. Perkins stopped me at the drugstore to say your tip about using vinegar to clean coffee stains from mugs changed her life. We could run another one of those instead."

"Sloan Jones," Myrtle said sternly. "Did you or did you not ask me to cover these murders?"

There was hesitation on the other end of the line. Apparently, Sloan wasn't at all sure that's what had transpired. Myrtle, instead, had assigned herself the story. "I guess so."

"And isn't the point of a newspaper to, you know, report the news?"

"In theory, yes."

"Then I suggest you print my article exactly as written. Red will just have to deal with it."

Sloan sighed deeply. "If Red storms in my office tomorrow, I might call you to talk with him."

"Gladly," said Myrtle. "Though I'll be busy investigating."

"Just be careful, would you? Two murders in Bradley is alarming enough without adding you to the count."

"How touching. You're concerned for my safety."

"I'm concerned about losing my best columnist," said Sloan. "Do you know how hard it is to find someone who can write three hundred words about using dryer sheets to repel mosquitoes?"

Myrtle snorted. "Flattery will get you nowhere, Sloan. Just print the article."

"Yes, ma'am," said Sloan resignedly. "It'll be in tomorrow's edition."

"Front page?" pressed Myrtle.

"Front page," confirmed Sloan.

Satisfied, Myrtle hung up and turned her attention to arranging a meeting with Gladys for the following day. While one was getting things knocked out, it seemed one should move to the next item on the list. Gladys answered on the first ring.

"Hello?" The voice was slightly anxious on the other end.

"Gladys, it's Myrtle Clover."

"Oh, hi Myrtle. I was just thinking about you. Your Jell-O salad was really creative."

"Thank you," said Myrtle. "I was wondering if you might be free for a chat tomorrow? Perhaps we could have coffee at your hotel. I haven't really had the opportunity to catch up."

"That would be really nice," said Gladys, sounding pleased. "I don't have any plans. What time works for you?"

"How about ten o'clock?"

"Perfect! I'll look forward to it."

Myrtle hung up, satisfied. Tomorrow, she would get to the bottom of Gladys's financial troubles and her supposed friendship with Belinda. If Frank was right, Gladys had been desperate for money, believing Belinda would leave her something in her will. Finding out that wasn't the case could certainly have been a motive for murder.

For her last phone call, she buzzed Miles, telling them they had a coffee date with Gladys. Miles seemed less than enthused by this announcement, but grudgingly offered to drive her there by ten.

Myrtle was ready and waiting when Miles pulled up in front of her house the next morning. She stepped out briskly, her cane thumping purposefully on the walkway.

"Good morning," said Miles. "I brought coffee." He nodded at two travel mugs in the cup holders.

"How thoughtful," said Myrtle, settling into the passenger seat. "Although a rather unusual thing to bring to a coffee date."

"After spending so much time at Greener Pastures yesterday, I thought the more coffee, the better."

"Yes. Such a horrid place. I had nightmares last night."

Miles pulled away from the curb. "At least we learned Harold might have had some issues with alcohol back in his working days. And more information about Belinda's involvement with the pain management clinic, of course."

"A vague rumor from Winston's deceased former roommate isn't exactly solid evidence," said Myrtle. "Nor is gossip from Winston. But it's a thread worth pulling. I'll agree it was useful learning more about Belinda's investment. With any luck, we'll learn more from Gladys, although I can't say I've ever been impressed with her intellect. We'll see what she has to say for herself."

The Bradley Inn lobby had beige wallpaper and floral print furniture from the 1990s. Or perhaps, the 1890s. Everything seemed very old. There was a small café area with wicker chairs and glass-topped tables where they found Gladys seated at a corner table with a view of the entrance. Complimentary coffee and stale mini-muffins were provided on a side table.

Gladys waved enthusiastically at them as they approached. She was wearing a floral blouse that was a size too small and a cardigan, despite the summer heat. She stood, giving Myrtle an unwanted hug and Miles a lingering handshake.

"Good to see you again, Miles," said Gladys, gushing. "I didn't really have a chance to talk at the memorial service. What a strong name you have! Were you named after someone in your family?"

Miles, accustomed to the widows and singles of Bradley throwing themselves mercilessly at him, gave her a polite response, explaining Miles was a surname in his family.

"Well, it's such a great name! How long have you two known each other? It's so nice to see such close friendship at our age." Gladys reached out and touched Miles on the arm.

The whole coffee had started out in a direction Myrtle hadn't anticipated. It was time to divert the course of the conversation. "Miles, let's grab a couple of coffees before we sit down."

Gladys looked a bit deflated. "Of course you should. And there are muffins over there, too."

The mini-muffins were just as desiccated up-close as they'd appeared at first. Both Myrtle and Miles passed on them altogether. "Is the coffee any good?" asked Miles dubiously in a low voice.

"All coffee is good if you put enough creamer and sugar in it." Myrtle, accordingly, dumped in copious amounts of both.

Miles said, "Perhaps we should create a signal, if one of us wants to leave."

"I'm assuming you're the one who might want to escape. Fine. Start whistling when you do."

Miles frowned. "Whistling? That doesn't seem quite subtle enough in the setting."

"I'm sure you can figure out a way to be unobtrusive."

Miles was considering this as they returned to the table.

"I'm so glad you're both here," said Gladys again. "You know how difficult it is to be alone at our age." She batted her few remaining eyelashes at Miles, who recoiled a bit and began whistling an old Ray Charles tune.

Myrtle ignored him. "You shouldn't be alone at all, should you? Millie Thatcher and Harold are here at the hotel."

Gladys nodded, but her eyes darkened. "Yes, but they're keeping to themselves. Especially Harold, even though I understand that. I think he'd feel better if he got out of his hotel room, though. I feel better being out of it." She gave Miles a shy look. "Do you like dancing?"

Miles looked startled. "Not really."

"Oh, no, that's a shame. I saw the community center has a senior dance night."

Miles started whistling a shaky rendition of "Moon River."

Myrtle ignored it again. Instead, she powered ahead with her interview of Gladys. "Speaking of Harold, what did you make of Evie? Did you know her well in school?"

Gladys gave her a blank look. "Evie? No I didn't know her at all. We weren't in the same classes."

Myrtle supposed not. It was really a wonder that Gladys wasn't held back a grade or two. And Evie had been a high-flyer, always on the honor roll. "And what did you make of her murder?"

"It's just horrible, isn't it? Awful. I could barely sleep last night, thinking about it." Gladys's voice was just a bit flat, which seemed to make her words a good deal less genuine.

"You must have had some sort of an opinion of her," said Myrtle, now impatient.

Gladys scrounged around in her brain for something to say. "She seemed like she was really devoted to Harold, didn't she?"

The lobby television suddenly sounded loudly in the adjacent room as the hosts on a shopping network oohed and ahhed over a bedazzled sweater.

Gladys reached in her purse. "I'm going to have a piece of gum. Would either of you like some?"

Myrtle cringed. She had an antipathy toward gum since her days as a teacher. The war on gum was a constant thing in the classroom.

Miles shook his head.

Gladys's rummaging managed to dislodge an overdue bill, which floated onto the table before wafting to the floor. Miles, ever the gentleman, picked it up and handed it politely to Gladys. She flushed a bit and took it quickly from him.

The gum refused to surface, but a gallon-sized bag filled with hotel toiletries, coffee packets, cups wrapped in plastic, and washcloths popped out. Gladys colored a bit more before stuffing it back in her tremendous purse. "Those lovely little soaps. They were just going to throw them away. And they're complimentary."

Myrtle highly doubted the washcloths were. "Gladys, is everything all right? I mean, personally? Are you doing okay?"

To Myrtle's dismay, this prompted Gladys to burst into tears. Myrtle, sure Gladys wouldn't be able to successfully retrieve tissues from the voluminous bag, hastily found her own and thrust the packet Gladys's way.

"Nothing is okay," wailed Gladys. "Everything is going wrong."

Myrtle tried to wait patiently until Gladys had calmed down enough to speak while Miles fidgeted with his coffee cup. The TV continued blasting more over-the-top gushing about the bedazzled sweater until Myrtle stomped over, found the errant remote, and muted the program. She returned to the table, where Gladys seemed to be getting hold of herself.

Gladys sighed. "I'm totally broke. I have one more credit card that hasn't been maxed out, and that's how I'll pay my bill here." She gave them an earnest look. "Belinda said she was going to take care of me. She was going to leave me money in her will. I promise she did."

"You were counting on that," said Myrtle.

Gladys nodded, sniffing. "Yeah. I mean, that and the lottery."

Myrtle and Miles exchanged a look. Myrtle said, "I'm not certain the lottery is a good financial strategy."

Gladys rubbed her eyes. Sadly, this smeared the eye makeup she had in place there. "I have a system, though. It's all based on my horoscope. So I do research."

It all sounded very similar to Winston's claim he had a system for bingo. Myrtle said sternly, "I know a real psychic who creates horoscopes, and she would be the first to say you don't need to play the lottery with it." She paused. "Going back to our previous subject. Where were you when poor Evie perished?"

Miles gave her a reproving look. Perhaps he thought she was running too roughshod over Gladys's feelings. Or that she was too accusatory. But Gladys didn't seem to notice.

"Oh, I was at the hotel. I like to sleep in when I can. This morning excepted, of course."

Myrtle was quite convinced she herself had never slept in until ten in the morning. Bouts of flu excepted, of course.

"Why do you think someone would murder Evie?" asked Gladys. "She never did anyone any harm."

But Myrtle didn't feel like floating theories. Instead, she said, "Last time we spoke, you thought Evie might have killed Belinda."

"True. But I guess she didn't, if she's dead now. Unless there are two killers. Gosh, do you think there might be?"

Myrtle did not. It seemed highly unlikely in a group of octogenarians. She said, "I'm not sure of anything, Gladys. But I'm interested in hearing more about why you thought Belinda was leaving you money. Somehow, I've gotten the impression that you haven't seen Belinda as much through the years."

Gladys blinked. "Did someone say that?"

"People talk."

Gladys said in a quiet voice, "I was always a good friend to her. *Always*. I'd have done anything for her, and that started in high school." She laughed. "I'd always be doing her homework for her."

Myrtle highly disapproved of this in every way. Firstly, she despised cheating. Secondly, she thought Belinda would have had the common sense to choose someone brighter than Gladys to complete her assignments for her.

Miles cleared his throat. "And later in life? You stayed in touch?"

Gladys looked delighted that Miles was addressing her. "We did! Of course, I had more free time than Belinda, so I was usually the one reaching out." She gave Miles a shy look. "Do you like pot roast? I make an incredible pot roast. It's always way too much for one person."

Miles colored, and Myrtle jumped back into the conversation before he started whistling again. "You were the one trying to keep up your friendship with Belinda, you were saying."

Gladys sighed. "Yes. But like I said, Belinda was busy."

"And how did you get the impression Belinda was going to leave you a legacy in her will?" asked Myrtle.

Gladys looked down at her cold coffee. "I guess it was just wishful thinking. I kept telling her it would be nice to get a little remembrance from her. Maybe I blew it up in my head."

Myrtle saw tears gathering once again in the corners of Gladys's eyes and hurried forward. "On a different topic, do you know much about Harold and his career?"

"He's an important doctor," said Gladys with a shrug. "He operated on people."

"He was a surgeon, yes. But have you heard anything negative about Harold or his practice?" pressed Myrtle.

Gladys shook her head. She seemed to still be dwelling on her supposed friendship with Belinda, perhaps coming to the realization that not only did Belinda leave her out of her will, but that they really hadn't been friends to begin with.

Myrtle was about to make an excuse so they could leave when Gladys said sadly, "The reunion wasn't what I thought it would be."

Myrtle supposed it hadn't. There had been a dead body to conclude the festivities.

Miles asked, "What was it like instead?"

Gladys heaved out a sigh. "Just not fun. I was nervous about seeing everybody after so long. I mean, I've changed a lot since high school."

"We've *all* changed since high school," said Myrtle.

"I know. But it was so overwhelming, you know? Just walking into the building made so many old memories come back. And everybody was so successful. It made me feel very small."

Miles said, "I'm not sure anyone feels good while attending a high school reunion."

"Have you been to one of yours?" asked Myrtle curiously.

Miles said, "My wife, Maeve, wanted to go to mine." He sighed. "She enjoyed herself a lot more than I did. When you don't have to remember anyone's name or pretend high school was fun, you can have a good time."

A hotel staff member walked over to the refreshments to clean the counter. Gladys said, "Ma'am? Can I have extra soap for my room?"

The woman gave her an exasperated look. "Room 312."

"Goodness, but you have a good memory."

Myrtle suspected it was the repetition of the request and not the excellence of the woman's memory that was key. She also suspected they weren't going to get much more from Gladys, who was starting to look even vaguer than she usually did.

"I think we should leave you be, dear," said Myrtle, standing up. Miles stood with relief, likely happy to avoid any further romantic overtures by Gladys.

"Oh, really?" Gladys looked disappointed. "I was hoping maybe we could hang out for a while."

This was decidedly not Myrtle's plan for the day. She'd rather be talking with Millie Thatcher and perhaps digging a bit on Harold. Then there was Frank, who had a truly excellent motive for ridding the world of Belinda. There was plenty to do, none of it involving Gladys.

"Another time, maybe," said Myrtle. "But we enjoyed our coffee with you, didn't we, Miles?"

Miles gave a stiff smile, which appeared to delight Gladys. She quickly rummaged in her purse again, dredging up a receipt. Another past-due bill wafted to the floor in the process. She jotted her phone number down on it and handed it to Miles, a wistful expression on her face. "In case you'd like to chat. Or meet up for more coffee."

Miles turned quite red again, taking the paper reluctantly. Ever the gentleman, he said, "Thank you."

Chapter Twenty-Three

Then they were off again. "That was excruciating," said Miles.

"It really wasn't that bad. You're just being sensitive."

Miles said, "I harbor no feelings whatsoever for Gladys."

"There simply aren't enough senior men for older ladies to cavort with, Miles. You know this. You're like a unicorn."

Miles muttered, "I don't feel like a unicorn." He paused. "I'm just driving in the general vicinity of our houses. Is there somewhere else we should be heading?"

"Home is fine." Myrtle's cell phone pinged at her, and she pulled it out, frowning at the device. "It's Elaine. She wants me to know she's left a 'care package' on my porch. Apparently, she found an incredible deal on pasta sauce."

Miles glanced over. "More spoils from her couponing adventures?"

"Twenty-four jars for ninety-eight cents, if you can believe it." Myrtle frowned. "The woman is turning into a hoarder. I'm not sure how Red is managing it."

"Speaking of Red," said Miles, "has he noticed the gnomes yet?"

A smile played around Myrtle's lips. "Oh yes. Dusty did a lovely job arranging them this time. I received a rather stern text message from Red, consisting entirely of capital letters. Apparently, the front yard looks like, and I quote, 'A GARDEN CENTER EXPLOSION.' Hopefully, he's not at home now. He sometimes is this time of day. I'd rather avoid him."

"Perhaps we should change course and stop by the library instead of going straight home. That way you can avoid any immediate confrontation."

"An excellent suggestion," said Myrtle. "Besides, I want to see what we can find out about Harold's medical mishap. The internet is bound to have something, if we can put in appropriate search terms. Or perhaps a librarian can help with our research, if we run into problems. It could be a search that's better at the library than at home."

Miles turned around, heading back for downtown Bradley. It appeared to be a quiet day there, and Miles found them a parking place in front of the building. A few minutes later, as they were walking toward the stairs, Pasha suddenly appeared from behind a bush, proudly carrying what appeared to be a small rodent.

Miles stepped back. "She does get around, doesn't she?"

"She has a knack for knowing where I am and where I'm heading," said Myrtle. "Though I wish she wouldn't bring her prizes along."

Pasha dropped the thankfully deceased mouse at Myrtle's feet and looked up expectantly.

"Brilliant Pasha! You keep trying to spur me to give hunting a go, don't you? I'm afraid I'd rather not. But I still appreciate you." She contemplated the deceased rodent. "What do we do about this?"

"Can't it just remain on the library's property?"

Myrtle shook her head. "And sadden some poor child who's just read *Stuart Little* or *The Tale of Despereaux*?"

Miles was already reluctantly pulling a tissue from his pocket when Pasha, unimpressed with Myrtle and Miles's reaction, carried her dead prey off into the woods.

Miles relaxed, but the thought of disposing of the creature made him take out his hand sanitizer, despite having had no contact with the animal. They walked into the library, which was full of natural light and positively teeming with books. At least, it was teeming for a library of its size.

They were greeted by a young man with sleeve tattoos and a neatly trimmed beard. His nametag read "Marcus."

"Hey there! Welcome to Bradley Public Library. Anything I can help you find today?" His voice was cheerful but appropriately modulated for the setting.

"We're researching something that happened locally," said Myrtle. "Specifically, we're searching for any information about medical incidents at County Memorial Hospital from thirty years ago to ten years ago." Myrtle thought this an appropriate span of time to learn exactly what had happened during the botched surgery of, presumably, the Jensen boy that the bingo woman had mentioned. It would have been most helpful, however, if the time span could have been narrowed down.

Marcus didn't bat an eye. "Research project?"

"Something like that," Myrtle replied.

"Follow me," said Marcus, leading them to a computer station in a quiet corner. "We've digitized all of the *Bradley Bugle* archives going back to 1945. Plus, we have access to the state medical board database and court records."

"That's very comprehensive," said Miles, pushing his glasses up his nose.

"We're small but mighty," Marcus grinned. "History major," he added by way of explanation. "I'm all about preserving the record." He pulled up the newspaper archive and showed them how to search. "If you need anything else, just wave. I'll be at the desk."

It didn't take long before Myrtle and Miles felt as if they were looking for a needle in a haystack. Harold apparently had been quite involved in the community, and there were numerous mentions of him in the newspaper.

"This is all very annoying," muttered Myrtle as she found yet another mention of Harold at some sort of charity event.

"It would be more helpful if we knew the name of the child in the botched surgery."

"Yes, Miles, I agree that *would* be helpful. But we're in the situation of trying to find that out. If only Harold hadn't been out in public as much as he was. It's very irritating."

Miles said, "Maybe we should look at the court records. Or the medical board database."

But those turned out to be dead ends, too. There was no mention of Harold in either.

Myrtle frowned. "I wonder if Harold's botched surgery was a secret."

"Then how did anyone know about it?"

"Gossip, like everything else around here," said Myrtle. "Maybe the governing body at the hospital didn't know anything about it. It never went to the courts or anything like that. Maybe it's something Belinda knew about."

"Blackmail?" asked Miles.

"That seems rather doubtful, doesn't it? Considering Belinda was a wealthy woman herself." Myrtle thought it through, her fingers tapping on the table. "Maybe Belinda wanted to expose Harold. Set things straight."

"Why on earth would she want to do that? She didn't seem to be that sort of person."

Myrtle said, "Well, maybe she was simply bored and wanted to stir the pot. Anyway, it's a motive, isn't it?" She paused. "You know, it's all like a pattern that I can't quite see."

"What is?"

"Belinda's actions. I believe what she did at the reunion led straight to her murder. But I can't figure out the framework," said Myrtle.

Miles said, "Let's make a chart with the suspects and their connections to Belinda."

"How very organized, Miles!"

"Except for the fact that I don't have any paper to write the chart on."

Myrtle said, "I'm sure that lovely Marcus has some. He's such a nice boy. I'll go ask him."

Marcus gave her a couple of sheets of paper from a legal pad, and Myrtle shoved them and a pen from her huge purse at him. Miles carefully wrote out the names: Frank, Harold, Gladys, and Millie.

Myrtle said slowly, "So Frank and Millie were wronged by Belinda, and she rewarded them in her will."

Miles carefully put a dollar sign next to each name.

Myrtle peered at the other names. "Then we have Harold and Gladys."

"Gladys was expecting money from Belinda," noted Miles helpfully.

"True. And Gladys is apparently in dire straits. However, from what we know, Belinda told Gladys at the reunion that she wasn't going to give her anything."

Miles said, "Maybe that's because Belinda felt she hadn't wronged her."

Myrtle frowned. "Maybe Belinda felt *Gladys* had wronged *her*."

"In what way?"

"We'd have to ask Gladys that," said Myrtle.

Miles immediately appeared uncomfortable. "Please tell me we're not going to see Gladys again. She might be a killer, and she appears to have a crush on me."

"I'll just give her a friendly little phone call," said Myrtle.

Miles again looked uncomfortable, this time at the thought of making a phone call in the quiet of the library, and Myrtle said, "Don't worry. I'll step outside. For heaven's sake, Miles, I do have some sense."

Myrtle strode out of the library, then removed her phone from her purse. Gladys answered immediately. "Myrtle? Were you thinking about another coffee date?"

"Oh, no dear, but thanks for the offer. Perhaps sometime later. There's something I've been stewing over, and I was hoping you could fill me in."

Gladys's voice now sounded doubtful. "I'm not sure I know anything about anything, Myrtle."

This was rather likely. But Myrtle was fairly sure Gladys would at least be able to offer helpful information on events in Gladys's own life. "It's about Belinda. You see, I'm under the impression she was angry about something—something that happened between the two of you."

There was a pause on the other end, then Gladys burst into tears. Myrtle said, "There, there, Gladys. It can't be that bad. I'm sorry to bring it up, but I'm working for the paper and I have to figure out what happened, you see? I'm the crime reporter."

Now Gladys sounded horrified. "You won't write this in the paper, will you?"

"No, of course not. It's to be used for background information only."

Gladys sniffled on the other end of the line. "Nobody was supposed to know about it."

"What happened?" asked Myrtle, a note of urgency in her voice.

More sniffling. "You won't tell the others? I mean, the ones who went to the reunion?"

"Not a word to them."

Gladys took a deep, shaky breath. "I borrowed a little money from Belinda."

"And didn't pay it back?"

Gladys said slowly, "She didn't know I'd taken it. Belinda took me on as her assistant for a while. I had a lot of bills, and I wasn't making ends meet. I just took a little to tide me over. I was going to pay her back."

"And she found out about it."

Gladys wailed on the other end, and Myrtle held the phone away from her ear. "Belinda was so mad at me. She fired me on the spot and got security to walk me to the door. Said she'd have the stuff in my desk shipped to me."

Myrtle said, "What made you think Belinda was going to include you in her will? Under these circumstances?"

There was silence on the line for a few moments before Gladys said meekly, "I thought she might be willing to let bygones be bygones. I guess she wasn't."

Myrtle said, "Did you get a formal invitation to the reunion?"

Another silence. Gladys said in a low voice, "No. I found out about it because Evie had put something on social media about it, and I followed her. I thought Belinda just overlooked me, so I came on." She sighed. "Then she wasn't very happy to see me."

Myrtle said, "I know this has been hard to talk about, but I thank you very much for the information, Gladys. It's been very useful."

Gladys sounded marginally more cheerful at the praise. "Okay. Thanks, Myrtle."

There was a spring to Myrtle's step as they walked toward the exit.

"Any luck?" asked Marcus from his station at the reference desk.

"Not a bit," said Myrtle. "Which has given us a bit of direction."

Marcus gave them a smile, although his expression said that he didn't understand.

They blinked in the sunlight outside for a minute before heading down the steep stairs for the parking lot. Next to Miles's car stood Millie Thatcher. She was fumbling with her keys while holding a thick stack of periodicals.

"Millie!" called Myrtle.

Millie nearly dropped the keys and the periodicals as she jumped. Seeing Myrtle and Miles, she relaxed somewhat, although she still looked wary. "What are you two doing here?" She was wearing the same clothes she'd worn at the memorial service and her hair was pulled back severely. Reading glasses hung from a chain around her neck. She clutched the magazines as though they were precious artifacts.

"Well, you know, we're book lovers. You can't keep us away from the library," said Myrtle. She glanced at Millie's stack of periodicals. "Some light reading?"

"Scientific journals. The hotel Wi-Fi is abysmal, and I wanted to catch up on my reading. The Bradley library is surprisingly well-outfitted."

Myrtle said, "I'm glad we ran into you. It's a good chance to catch up, isn't it? And there are those nice benches over there."

Millie cast a longing look at her scientific journals. "Well—"

Myrtle said in her most persuasive voice, "The benches are the kind that have backs on them. Come on, Millie. You can read later. Plenty more hours in the day."

"Okay," she said reluctantly. She shoved the journals into her car, locked it again, and then allowed herself to be led to the benches.

Apparently, Millie wasn't in any mood for small talk. "Have the police made any progress with the investigation?" she asked.

"Oh, I wouldn't know that," said Myrtle.

"Wouldn't you? I thought your son was the police chief."

Myrtle said, "Yes, but Red doesn't discuss his work. And he doesn't want me anywhere near a murder investigation. It's quite aggravating." She paused. "What do you make of Evie's death?"

Millie considered this. "She was a very intelligent woman. Evie was the only person who could match me in calculus. She seemed brilliant in a very quiet way, you know? Not showy, but precise. She should have been a mathematician."

"I didn't realize she was so good at the subject. Perhaps because math wasn't my area of expertise," said Myrtle.

"She was. And she chose a teaching career when she should have gone into research. It always struck me as a waste of her analytical mind." Millie shrugged. "People always seemed to underestimate her because she was so pleasant and accommodating. That was their mistake. She was always the smartest woman in the room. Aside from me, of course."

"You kept up with Evie then?" asked Miles. "Through the years?"

Millie looked surprised, as if she'd forgotten Miles was there. "No, not really. We weren't friends in school because we were so competitive with each other for earning the top grades."

"And yet you set up a time to walk with Evie the morning she died," said Myrtle.

"What? I certainly didn't. Why would I do such a thing?"

"To catch up?" suggested Myrtle. "Haven't the police asked you about it?"

"They did and I sent them away with a flea in their ear. It's simply not true," said Millie.

Myrtle asked, "So you weren't at the high school when Evie died?"

"No. I was at the diner having an early breakfast and reading. Asimov, if you must know."

Myrtle and Miles looked at each other. "That's interesting," said Myrtle. "Because *we* were at the diner having an early breakfast. We didn't see you there."

"I must have left by the time you got there," said Millie stiffly. "Are you accusing me of something, Myrtle?"

"I wouldn't dream of it."

"Why would I arrange exercise with someone I haven't seen in decades?" asked Millie.

"Because you haven't seen her in decades," said Myrtle dryly. "Are you sure you didn't mention something to Evie in passing? Then forgot about it?"

"My memory is perfect. And if I'd made arrangements, which I wouldn't have, I would have put them right in my planner."

Myrtle looked thoughtfully at her. "Maybe the misunderstanding was on Evie's end."

"Why not? It's a common problem for people our age."

Myrtle said, "Have you had any other thoughts about Belinda's death?"

"I've always tried not to waste too much thought on Belinda. She wasn't worth my time," said Millie in a clipped voice.

Miles cleared his throat. "It must have stung for Belinda to steal your project. You must have put a lot of time into it."

"You don't know the half of it. Even worse, it kept me from ever really trusting anyone again." Millie reached into her purse, pulling out an elderly leather wallet. From the billfold section, she took out a laminated newspaper story.

Chapter Twenty-Four

Myrtle and Miles peered at the old newspaper clipping. "It's an article on Belinda's science fair win," said Myrtle. "So you clearly do remember the incident, after all. When I asked you about it before, you claimed to have no idea what I was talking about."

Millie said, "You work for the newspaper, which didn't make me exactly want to open up to you. It's a painful topic to revisit. But right now, I'm ready to escape Bradley. Maybe you can figure out what happened to Belinda and Evie, and I can finally go back home."

"Why would you carry something like that article around with you?"

"As a reminder," said Millie curtly. "I've always been very careful not to be too trusting of others ever again."

Miles looked at her sadly.

"Don't pity me," she said to him, head held high.

Miles shifted his gaze.

"I'm not going to say it didn't rankle. Do you know what it's like to have your life's potential ripped away from you? I could have used that science fair research to jumpstart other research that would have proven groundbreaking. Instead, it was just a footnote in Belinda's college application. It derailed my entire career."

"And you never saw Belinda? Never ran into her after high school?" asked Myrtle.

Millie said, "Only once. It was at a medical conference. I was attending as a researcher. Belinda was attending as an investor in some sort of medical facility. Basically, she was being wined and dined." She paused. "Harold was there too, as a matter of fact. I didn't speak with either one of them. I got the impression they didn't even recognize me."

Myrtle believed it. Millie had changed a lot since high school, and not in the best way. "Where was the conference?"

"Charlotte. So not too far away, which is probably why both of them were there. They *did* spend time together, so I guess they recognized each other."

Myrtle raised her eyebrows. "Was there a romantic connection, then?"

"There might have been, although Harold had to drive back home at one point because he was called into work. I didn't care and wasn't tracking what they were doing. But they were both drinking a lot. Harold was sloppy drunk and Belinda wasn't too far behind." Millie pressed her lips together. "I thought it was disgraceful to behave that way at a work event."

Myrtle said, "One other question for you. Did you ever hear anything about Gladys? Or maybe Frank?"

"Nothing more than what I told you the first time. Gladys has financial problems. Frank was angry about a clinic that Belinda was somehow involved in." Millie shrugged again. "That's all I know. But Frank was definitely angry when he was talking to Belinda. Maybe he did it."

"Would he murder Evie, though?"

Millie said, "Who knows?"

"It seems to me you're the one who should know more about what happened to Belinda than anyone else," said Myrtle. "After all, you were all over the school winning the scavenger hunt."

Millie looked irritated. "I've already told what little I saw. I certainly didn't see anyone leaving the scene of the crime or anything like that. I was focused on winning."

It seemed to Myrtle that winning was the common thread in Millie's goals. She said, "It didn't have to be something so blatantly obvious. Perhaps it's something just run-of-the-mill. A small detail. Something that didn't quite fit in."

Millie was looking at Myrtle as if she thought *Myrtle* was something that didn't quite fit in. "Really, there's nothing."

Miles cleared his throat. "How about Winston? Did you see Winston during the hunt?"

Millie frowned. "Winston? I haven't thought much about Winston. He seems so very innocuous."

"Did you see him during the scavenger hunt?" he asked mildly.

"I suppose I did," Millie said slowly. "Only for a second. He was trying to catch up with Belinda, but she waved him away dismissively with her hand. I remember thinking that was par for the course with Belinda. Even back in high school, she could make people feel low."

"Did you hear any of their conversation? What they might have been talking about?" asked Miles.

"Nope. But I figured Winston was probably embarrassing himself by trying to flirt with Belinda. That's his modus operandi, after all. I briefly thought that naturally she'd be brushing him off if he was hitting on her." Millie paused. "But it could have been for other reasons."

Myrtle, who had been trying to get the conversation back to other suspects, was suddenly more interested. "Is there more to Winston that meets the eye? You just finished telling us how innocuous he was."

Millie looked annoyed. She was clearly someone who disliked being contradicted. "Well, he *is* innocuous. Unless you worked with him."

Myrtle was trying and failing to remember what Winston Rouse had done for a living. Millie looked smug at knowing information Myrtle didn't. "He was a lawyer. I looked him up online before the reunion and discovered he'd been disbarred."

"Really?" Myrtle attempted to square a disbarment with the Winston she was acquainted with.

"That's right. I dug a little deeper and found out it was because he'd mishandled client funds."

"How on earth did you find that out?" asked Myrtle.

"I'm a researcher, remember? I came across state bar association records that confirm he was disbarred. He commingled personal funds with client trust accounts." Millie looked impatiently at Myrtle and Miles for not immediately catching on. "He used client settlement money to temporarily cover his own financial shortcomings."

"My, my," said Myrtle. There was more to Winston than she'd originally thought. "So you're thinking Belinda found out."

"Belinda had quite an extensive network. People talk," said Millie.

Myrtle and Miles glanced at each other. Since Belinda had clearly intended retribution for those she thought should pay the piper, it could be that Winston wanted to eliminate Belinda before she ruined his cozy, benign existence at the retirement home.

Millie looked at her watch. "Now, if that's all, I'd like to get back to the hotel. I have some reading to do."

Myrtle and Miles watched as Millie quickly got into her car and drove away. Then they climbed into Miles's sedan to head back to Myrtle's house.

Myrtle felt ornery. "I never did like that Millie. So supercilious."

"That's a side effect of being very smart. I get the opinion Millie is very smart."

"Yes, but does she have to rub it in everyone's face? I have the feeling Millie isn't exactly overrun with friends," said Myrtle with a sniff.

Miles said, "You didn't tell me what happened with your phone call with Gladys."

"Oh, I forgot when we saw Millie in the parking lot. I think we're onto something with Belinda and her wishes for both reparations and retribution. Gladys had embezzled money from Belinda when she'd worked for her. A strikingly similar story to Winston's."

Miles arched his eyebrows. "I wouldn't have thought Gladys the type."

"I got the impression she really didn't think she'd done anything wrong. It's clear Belinda felt differently. Gladys also admitted that she'd crashed the reunion, herself. She received no invitation from Belinda."

As Miles turned onto Magnolia Drive, Myrtle gasped, a sound that made Miles brake the car hard.

"What is it?" asked Miles, scanning the road for a pet, or perhaps a small child.

"Puddin! She's at my house. It must be the end of the world."

Miles was simply relieved he hadn't been about to run over something or someone. "Let's not gasp while I'm driving. It's very alarming."

"I want to find out what she's doing at my house when she's always so reluctant to be there. She must have an ulterior motive."

Puddin gave Myrtle a simpering smile as they drove into the driveway.

"Puddin? What an unexpected surprise," said Myrtle curtly.

"Ain't it? Thought I'd just run by real quick-like." Puddin's pale face looked odd with the phony smile pasted on it.

"May I ask why I've been granted the pleasure of your company?"

"Just thought I'd say hi," said Puddin.

Miles said, "I'll let the two of you have a nice visit. See you later, Myrtle."

Myrtle gave him an absentminded wave as he drove away. "What's the real reason you're here?"

Puddin looked exasperated. "Dusty tole me to come back and do more work here. I couldn't work much last week because my back was thrown."

Myrtle had concluded Puddin's back was quite aerobic indeed. It was always leaping around, throwing itself, and always at the worst possible times. "I suppose money is the motivating factor?"

Puddin screwed up her face in a most unattractive manner. "Speak English."

"You need money."

Puddin shrugged. "Phone bill needs payin."

"Did you bring your own cleaning supplies?" Myrtle looked vainly around for the missing supplies.

"You got 'em," said Puddin with yet another shrug as she followed Myrtle inside.

Myrtle gave Puddin a bit of direction with the chores that needed completing. Myrtle suspected not much cleaning would actually be accomplished. That was because Puddin appeared to be in a chatty mood.

Puddin slowly pushed a dust cloth on the top of a table. "You been workin' on that murder again?"

"Two murders, actually. Yes."

Puddin perked up. "Another body?"

"That's correct."

Puddin said, "Dusty was talkin' to me about one of them guys. Howard."

"Harold?" Myrtle perked up a bit. Puddin rarely knew anything interesting, but Dusty might. And Puddin was always eager to share what she knew. "Does Dusty do yard work for

Harold? I'd have thought that would be out of his way. They're in the county, not the town limits." Myrtle also suspected Harold had too much money and sense to use Dusty for his yard.

"No, he ain't his yardman. But Dusty done worked at the hospital where the guy worked."

Myrtle frowned. "Dusty? Working at a hospital? In what capacity?" She was absolutely certain any hospital wouldn't employ Dusty for landscaping purposes.

"You know he used to do maintenance stuff."

"Vaguely," said Myrtle.

"Well, he did for the hospital."

"Must have been a while back," said Myrtle. But then, Dusty wasn't exactly a young man.

"It was," said Puddin. "An' he knew that Harold. He said he'd be drinkin' a lot." Puddin looked very self-righteous. Apparently, drinking wasn't one of Puddin's vices. At least, she didn't qualify her own drinking as an issue.

"He came in smellin' like booze a lot," said Puddin viciously.

Myrtle leaned forward on her cane. "Did Dusty hear of any issues that Harold's drinking caused? Any sort of problem when he was working?"

"Yep. Said Harold killed a boy during an operation." Puddin shook her head.

"Did Dusty have any information about it?"

Puddin gave her a scornful look. "Dusty ain't a doctor. He didn't know nothing about the operation. He just knew Harold was smelling like booze before he done it."

Which was precisely the information Myrtle had been looking for. The fact that it came from this particular source was quite astonishing.

"Think he done killed them two people?" asked Puddin.

"I have no idea," said Myrtle. "There are other suspects who are equally capable. I'll have to do more digging." She frowned. "How did you come about this information?"

"I done told you! Dusty said."

"Yes, but what made Harold Blackwood come up in the first place?" asked Myrtle.

Puddin gave her a sullen look. "Other people talkin' about him. Said he was there at that party."

"The reunion."

"Whatever," said Puddin. "Anyway, it made him remember that." She paused. "Was he drunk at the party? The reunion?"

"He didn't seem to be." Myrtle could tell Puddin had run out of interesting information. "Keep dusting."

Puddin started lackadaisically dusting once more while Myrtle texted Miles that she had information on Harold. She waited impatiently for a reply, but none came. Myrtle reached the discouraging conclusion that Miles had likely fallen asleep.

"Dustin' is done," said Puddin.

Myrtle stood up, looking carefully at her surfaces. "I think not."

"I don't see nuthin.'"

"Anything. You don't see anything," said Myrtle.

"Glad you agree with me."

Myrtle gritted her teeth. "You didn't dust the kitchen table."

"Ain't no dust on it."

"There *isn't* any dust on it," said Myrtle.

"Then we're good," said Puddin. "Just need some money."

"Which I'll be happy to provide, if you finish the job and do more work. For heaven's sake, you haven't done anything at all."

"Done told you stuff for your story," said Puddin sullenly.

"I don't pay my informants."

Puddin heaved a dramatic sigh. "I'm gonna tell Dusty it's up to him to make the money. Don't got the patience for this. She headed for the front door. "What's this stuff?" she asked, pushing her foot into a couple of brown paper bags.

"Likely some of Elaine's couponing finds," said Myrtle with irritation. "Bring them in, will you?"

Puddin rolled her eyes and leaned forward to pick one of them up. She made a jerking motion and howled. "My back!"

"Don't tell me. It's thrown."

Puddin shot her a mutinous look. "It is!"

"Never mind, just leave it on the front porch. I'm sure some-one will bring it in for me later." Myrtle was ready to be done with Puddin for the day. In fact, she was rather ready to be done with everyone for the day.

Chapter Twenty-Five

For a while, it was quite peaceful in Myrtle's home. She completed a crossword puzzle, finished a sudoku, and ate a snack. Annoyingly, there was no response from Miles regarding her text. His nap was going on ridiculously long, something that made Myrtle quite envious. She was never a good napper and woke up feeling as if she'd been run over.

When there was a knock at her door, Myrtle walked curiously over. Harold Blackburn was there.

"Harold?" she asked. "Everything okay?"

"Not really," he said. "It's hard to adjust without Evie." He sighed. "Honestly, I've been looking for something to divert myself. We aren't allowed to leave town yet, and there's not much to keep my mind off what happened. I was wondering if I could trouble you for a few minutes of your time. I've already visited Winston over at the retirement home." He gave another sigh. "I'm not sure I want to visit with Millie. She's always so prickly."

Myrtle took pride in her own prickliness. It made her like Millie a bit more, although not by much. Her smugness was anathema to Myrtle. "Would you like something to drink?"

"No, but I wouldn't turn down a little food." Harold settled down at Myrtle's kitchen table with surprising comfort.

It was all fairly insufferable. Myrtle supposed Evie must have served Harold food every day of her life. Evie and she had consumed the cookies she usually had for Jack, so those were gone. Myrtle opened her fridge and cast a dubious look at the contents. She spotted a tuna casserole she'd made from some of the cans of tuna fish Elaine had given her. She hadn't had the chance to consume it herself. It would do in a pinch. She'd also used some of Elaine's condensed milk since she'd been out of evaporated milk—a substitution she now questioned as the casserole had acquired a rather sweet aroma.

While Harold chatted about the hotel and how Bradley had changed, Myrtle heated up a large glob of the casserole and gave it to Harold.

"Thank you, Myrtle." Harold took a big bite, chewed a few times, then had a surprised expression cross his features. His jaw seemed to stop working momentarily. "Napkin," he muttered, his voice tight.

Myrtle thrust a napkin at him. He paused with his chewing, then gestured wildly toward the living room window. "Someone's coming!"

Myrtle frowned and moved toward the front door. Looking out the window, she said, "No one's there, Harold. Perhaps you're hallucinating."

When she returned, Harold had somehow managed to finish chewing and his napkin was suspiciously bulky. He shoved it quickly into his pocket, his face a strange shade of green. Harold cleared his throat and seemed determined to find a subject to talk about. "Have you heard from your Red when we might be able to leave town? Not you, of course, but our other classmates?"

"No, Red and I don't chat about his cases." It was an understatement comparable to saying the Atlantic Ocean was damp.

Harold looked disappointed, and Myrtle felt that had been the entire reason for his visit. He stared down at the remaining glob of tuna salad as if it were a particularly gruesome crime scene. "You know," he said carefully, "I'm not sure that I'm all that hungry, after all. It's the grief, you see. It really affects my appetite."

"That would be most inconvenient."

Myrtle's phone made a few bleats to indicate a text message had finally come through. "You have info on Harold?" it asked. "What is it?"

Unfortunately, Myrtle's phone was on the kitchen table. Equally unfortunately, Harold was attempting to look anywhere but at the glob of tuna casserole. He froze after reading the message, his eyes widening first in shock, then narrowing in calculation. He turned those narrowed eyes her way.

Chapter Twenty-Six

Myrtle froze, too. There was hatred in Harold's eyes—the same look she'd seen in countless high schoolers when she'd assigned surprise tests. She stood up, wobbling a little. Harold tried to grab her arm, but was too slow. Myrtle was already moving for the front door, leaning heavily on her cane but moving with surprising speed for someone her age.

Fortunately, Harold didn't seem to be the quickest octogenarian around, either, but he was starting to catch up, his footsteps surprisingly nimble.

"Don't be ridiculous, Myrtle!" he called after her, his voice no longer frail. "I just want to explain!"

She got out the door, slamming it behind her. Spotting one of Elaine's bags on the porch, she somehow managed to lug the heavy package of canned goods in front of the door, silently thanking Elaine for her extreme shopping habit.

Myrtle hazarded a look behind her and saw Harold fly out the front door and immediately fall over the bags. Myrtle heard him cursing behind her, then silence. She looked across the street and saw Elaine's minivan was gone, as was the police cruiser. Her heart jumped as she heard her back door slam.

"Any port in a storm," she muttered, recalling Wanda's prophecy. She moved as fast as she could toward Erma's house, her cane tapping a desperate rhythm on the pavement.

Just as she reached Erma's walkway, she heard the side gate to her yard creak open. Harold was cutting through the yard, moving faster than any distinguished retired surgeon had the right to.

Myrtle pounded on Erma's door with the handle of her cane. "Erma! Open up!"

Erma opened the door and gaped at her, her rodentesque features even more pronounced than usual. "Myrtle Clover! What on earth—"

"Let me in, for heaven's sake!" Myrtle pushed past her, nearly knocking Erma over in her haste. "Lock the door!"

"What is going on?" Erma demanded, but she locked the door anyway, her natural nosiness overriding any objection to Myrtle's invasion. "Are you having some kind of episode?"

Harold appeared on the walkway, his distinguished appearance now marred by a wild look in his eyes and Myrtle's garden soil on his tweed jacket. He spotted Myrtle through Erma's front window and approached the door.

"Is that Dr. Blackwood?" Erma peered through the window. "My goodness, he certainly moves well for his age! Should I let him in? He looks upset."

"Absolutely not!" Myrtle grabbed Erma's wrist with surprising strength. "He's trying to kill me."

"Kill you?" Erma's eyes widened with delight. "Are you certain? That sounds rather far-fetched."

The doorbell rang, making both women jump.

"Ladies?" Harold called, his voice eerily calm. "I believe there's been a misunderstanding. I'd just like a word with Myrtle."

"A word and a blunt object to my head," muttered Myrtle. She looked around frantically. "Where's your phone?"

"Myrtle," Harold called again, "don't you think you're overreacting? Let's talk about this like adults."

"Like adults?" Erma whispered, clearly thrilled by the unfolding drama. "What exactly happened between you two? Is this some sort of lover's quarrel?"

"For heaven's sake, Erma. The man is a murderer." Myrtle hissed. "He killed two women, and now he's after me."

"Hot diggity!" Erma clutched her heart, her expression suggesting this was the most exciting thing to happen to her in years. "My phone is in the kitchen. Should I call the police or get my dad's old shotgun from the attic?"

"The police, Erma! Call Red!"

Harold was now trying the doorknob, his patience clearly wearing thin.

Erma scurried toward the kitchen but stopped abruptly. "I just remembered the neighborhood watch protocol."

"The what?"

Without explanation, Erma grabbed a brass candlestick from her mantle and rushed to a window. She threw it open and began shrieking at the top of her lungs while banging the candlestick against a cast-iron skillet that had appeared from nowhere.

"HELP! MURDER! INTRUDER! BINGO HAS BEEN CANCELED! I REPEAT—BINGO HAS BEEN CAN-

CELED!" she bellowed, her braying voice carrying across the entire neighborhood.

Harold immediately backed away from the door, looking alarmed.

"What on earth are you doing?" Myrtle demanded, torn between horror and admiration.

"The neighborhood watch alarm," Erma explained proudly between shrieks. "We developed it after Mabel Fitzwilliam's bridge club was interrupted by a raccoon. Everyone on the street knows to call the police when they hear it."

Sure enough, doors were opening up and down the street. Neighbors emerged, some brandishing phones, others with various household implements that could double as weapons. Mrs. Peterson from three houses down was already on her phone, gesturing wildly.

Harold, realizing he was now the center of attention for the entire neighborhood, retreated further. He looked desperately from Myrtle to the gathering crowd, then began backing toward the street.

"Don't let him get away!" Myrtle called out the window.

As if on cue, a large black shape darted between Harold's legs. Pasha, appearing from nowhere as she often did, tangled herself between his ankles. Harold stumbled, arms windmilling, before landing hard on a small patch of weedy marigolds.

"My flowers!" Erma wailed, momentarily forgetting the emergency.

"Your flowers will recover," Myrtle snapped. "Unlike Belinda and Evie."

Harold, looking disheveled and defeated, sat up in the crushed hydrangeas. "This is ridiculous," he muttered. "I'm a respected surgeon."

"Who operated while drunk and killed that little boy," Myrtle called out the window, her journalistic instincts taking over. "Isn't that right, Harold?"

A hush fell over the gathering crowd. Harold's face went white.

"You don't know what you're talking about," he said, but his voice lacked conviction.

"I think you'll find that I do," said Myrtle.

Harold's shoulders sagged. "It was an accident," he said quietly. "I'd had a few drinks at a conference. Belinda was there, as well. I didn't think I was impaired. The boy had appendicitis—it should have been routine."

Myrtle said in an ominous voice, "You should never have attempted that surgery. It not only led to the poor boy's death, it led to Belinda and Evie's deaths, too."

"I never intended for any of this to happen," Harold said, his professional demeanor crumbling. "Belinda always knew about the surgery. She and I drank too much at the conference—this was many years ago. Then I got called to the hospital—quite a drive from Charlotte. Later, Belinda put two and two together when the paper printed the boy's obituary. She cornered me at the reunion and said she was setting things right before she died. She wanted to tell the truth about what happened to my patient."

He continued. "She told me she was going to contact the medical board, have my case reopened. All those years of building my reputation would be gone. When I saw that paint can in the art room, I just reacted."

"And Evie?" pressed Myrtle.

"Evie knew me better than anyone. She saw the change in me after Belinda's death. Plus, she saw me leaving the art room that day. She didn't confront me immediately—that wasn't Evie's way. But later, she asked questions. She always was more perceptive than people gave her credit for."

"And what about Millie's supposed meeting with Evie at the track?" Myrtle asked.

A flicker of something—perhaps shame—crossed Harold's face. "There was no meeting. I made that up when I realized you were investigating. I thought it would direct suspicion toward Millie." He looked away.

The wail of a police siren cut through the air. Red's cruiser screeched to a halt in front of Erma's house, followed closely by another police car. Red jumped out, his face a mask of confusion as he took in the scene: Harold sitting in crushed hydrangeas, Erma still brandishing her candlestick, and Myrtle leaning out the window like a general surveying the battlefield.

"What in tarnation—" Red began.

"Your mother almost got murdered!" Erma shrieked gleefully before Myrtle could speak. "I saved her with my emergency alert system."

Red looked from Erma to his mother, his expression suggesting this was exactly the kind of chaos he expected to find whenever Myrtle was involved.

"What have you gotten yourself into now, Mama?" he asked wearily.

"Nothing I couldn't handle," Myrtle said with dignity. "With a little help from Erma and Pasha."

Pasha, looking extraordinarily pleased with herself, was now sitting on Harold's lap, effectively pinning him to the ground. She began calmly washing her paw.

"That cat," Harold muttered, "is the devil incarnate."

"Perhaps, when she's in the mood. She's a good judge of character," Myrtle replied. Then, turning to Red, she added, "You might want to ask Dr. Blackwood here about Belinda and Evie. And about a surgery he performed while under the influence—a botched appendectomy."

Red's eyebrows shot up. "Is that true, Dr. Blackwood?"

Harold looked around at the assembled neighbors, all watching with rapt attention. His shoulders slumped further.

"I think," he said quietly, "I'd like to speak with my attorney."

As the officers helped Harold to his feet and led him toward the police car, Red turned to his mother. "Mama, we need to talk about this."

"Later, dear," Myrtle said airily. "Right now, I need to call Miles. And then Sloan. This is front-page news."

"And I need to make coffee!" Erma declared. "For everyone! This is the most excitement we've had since Tippy's purse-dog got loose in the Nativity scene!"

As the neighbors swarmed into Erma's house, eager for details, Myrtle found herself in the unusual position of being grateful for Erma's love of gossip.

"One cup," she said grudgingly to Erma. "Then I really must write my article."

"Of course, of course," Erma nodded, her eyes gleaming. "But first, tell everyone how you figured it all out."

Myrtle settled into Erma's most comfortable chair, finding she didn't mind being the center of attention just this once.

Just as Myrtle was settling into Erma's armchair to begin her story, the crowd parted to reveal a disheveled Miles rushing up the walkway, looking frantically from the police cars to the gathered neighbors. Another police vehicle pulled to the side of the road and Shaw got out, striding purposefully toward Erma's house behind Miles.

"Myrtle!" Miles called, his voice tight with concern. "I just got your messages! I dozed off and—" He stopped short when he saw her comfortably ensconced in Erma's living room. "You're okay?" Miles looked as though he suspected Myrtle might have had a small stroke, considering she was willingly in Erma's house.

"Miles Bradford," Erma announced to the assembled crowd. "Always showing up after the excitement's over."

"I'm perfectly fine," Myrtle said. "Though no thanks to your napping habits. I've already caught the murderer while you were dead to the world."

Miles adjusted his glasses, which had gone slightly askew in his rush. "I can see that. I suppose my sidekick services weren't needed after all."

"On the contrary," Myrtle replied. "Your text message was what tipped Harold off. It was quite useful, just not in the way you intended."

Shaw looked from Harold in the police car to Myrtle in the armchair, his expression shifting from suspicion to grudging respect.

"I see," he said finally. "Well, Mrs. Clover, it appears I may have misjudged you."

"Happens to the best of us, dear," Myrtle said magnanimously. "Though ordinarily not to me."

Shaw folded his arms, his professional curiosity clearly overriding his pride. "Walk me through your thought process, Mrs. Clover. How did you narrow it down to Dr. Blackwood?"

The gathered neighbors leaned in, eager to hear Myrtle's explanation. Even Red moved closer.

Myrtle warmed to the opportunity. "It was a pattern, not a single clue. First, there was the alleged drinking problem. Winston's former roommate at Greener Pastures mentioned it, then my housekeeper, Puddin, confirmed her husband Dusty had worked maintenance at the hospital and seen Harold arrive smelling of alcohol."

"Surely that was decades ago," Shaw pointed out.

"Yes, but Belinda was about setting things right before she died. She was terminally ill, you see. She'd left money in her will to both Millie and Frank, who were people she'd wronged. It suggested she was clearing her conscience." Myrtle tapped her cane as she made her points.

Red was nodding now, following her logic, his expression shifting from exasperation to grudging admiration.

"Also telling was Harold's claim that Millie had arranged to meet Evie at the track—a meeting Millie vehemently denied. Harold was creating false leads." Myrtle's eyes narrowed. "And

Millie mentioned seeing Harold and Belinda together at a medical conference years ago, both drinking heavily. The pieces aligned when I learned about a surgery gone wrong involving a young boy. It turned out the surgery directly followed the conference."

"The final confirmation came when Harold saw Miles's text message about having information on him. His entire demeanor shifted instantly." Myrtle concluded. "Innocent people don't immediately try to corner elderly ladies in their homes."

Shaw cleared his throat, visibly uncomfortable as several neighbors murmured in agreement. "I owe you an apology, Mrs. Clover," he said, loud enough for everyone to hear. "I spent more time investigating you than considering you might be right."

A ripple of satisfied whispers spread through the crowd. Erma looked positively delighted.

"You should have listened to Lieutenant Perkins," Myrtle replied. "He warned you about me, didn't he?"

Shaw's ears reddened noticeably. "He mentioned you had an uncanny ability to solve cases, yes."

"And yet you dismissed me as a meddling old woman," Myrtle said, not bothering to hide her satisfaction.

Shaw tugged uncomfortably at his collar. "Mrs. Clover, the department would appreciate your formal statement. And perhaps, well . . . " He hesitated, glancing at Red before continuing. "Your perspective on any other aspects of the case we might have overlooked."

Red's eyebrows shot up in surprise, and he gave Shaw a look that suggested the detective had just joined some exclusive club of the humbled.

"Why, Detective Shaw," Myrtle said with exaggerated sweetness, "are you asking for my help?"

"Just a professional consultation," Shaw clarified, though everyone present could see his discomfort. "Given your obviously thorough understanding of the situation."

"I should get back to the station," Shaw said, nodding curtly to Myrtle. "We'll need to process Dr. Blackwood and take formal statements from everyone. I'll be in touch, Mrs. Clover."

As Shaw headed toward his vehicle, Red leaned down to his mother. "One of these days, you're going to give me a heart attack with these stunts."

"Nonsense," said Myrtle, her eyes following Shaw's retreating form with satisfaction. "Your heart is as strong as mine. It's practically a family trait."

"Tell us what happened," urged Erma, not to be denied her gossip.

"I just did," said Myrtle.

"No, no, the *long* version with all the details."

"All right. It all started when I crashed my high school reunion," Myrtle announced to her rapt audience. "Which just goes to show you should never exclude the brightest person in the class."

About the Author

Bestselling cozy mystery author Elizabeth Spann Craig is a library-loving, avid mystery reader. A pet-owning Southerner, her four series are full of cats, corgis, and cheese grits. The mother of two, she lives with her husband, a fun-loving corgi, and a couple of cute cats.

Sign up for Elizabeth's free newsletter to stay updated on releases:

https://bit.ly/2xZUXqO

This and That

I love hearing from my readers. You can find me on Facebook as Elizabeth Spann Craig Author, on Twitter as elizabethscraig, on my website at elizabethspanncraig.com, and by email at elizabethspanncraig@gmail.com.

Thanks so much for reading my book...I appreciate it. If you enjoyed the story, would you please leave a short review on the site where you purchased it? Just a few words would be great. Not only do I feel encouraged reading them, but they also help other readers discover my books. Thank you!

Did you know my books are available in print and ebook formats? Most of the Myrtle Clover series is available in audio and some of the Southern Quilting mysteries are. Find the audiobooks here: https://elizabethspanncraig.com/audio/

Please follow me on BookBub for my reading recommendations and release notifications.

I'd also like to thank some folks who helped me put this book together. Thanks to my cover designer, Karri Klawiter, for her awesome covers. Thanks to my editor, Judy Beatty for her help. Thanks to beta readers Amanda Arrieta, Rebecca Wahr, Cassie Kelley, and Dan Harris for all of their helpful suggestions and careful reading. Thanks to my ARC readers for helping to spread the word. Thanks, as always, to my family and readers.

Other Works by Elizabeth

Myrtle Clover Series in Order (be sure to look for the Myrtle series in audio, ebook, and print):

Pretty is as Pretty Dies

Progressive Dinner Deadly

A Dyeing Shame

A Body in the Backyard

Death at a Drop-In

A Body at Book Club

Death Pays a Visit

A Body at Bunco

Murder on Opening Night

Cruising for Murder

Cooking is Murder

A Body in the Trunk

Cleaning is Murder

Edit to Death

Hushed Up

A Body in the Attic

Murder on the Ballot

Death of a Suitor

A Dash of Murder
Death at a Diner
A Myrtle Clover Christmas
Murder at a Yard Sale
Doom and Bloom
A Toast to Murder
Mystery Loves Company
A Murder Down Memory Lane

THE VILLAGE LIBRARY Mysteries in Order:
Checked Out
Overdue
Borrowed Time
Hush-Hush
Where There's a Will
Frictional Characters
Spine Tingling
A Novel Idea
End of Story
Booked Up
Out of Circulation
Shelf Life
Dead Silence (2025)
The Sunset Ridge Mysteries in Order
The Type-A Guide to Solving Murder
The Type-A Guide to Dinner Parties
The Type-A Guide to Natural Disasters (2025)

Southern Quilting Mysteries in Order:

Quilt or Innocence

Knot What it Seams

Quilt Trip

Shear Trouble

Tying the Knot

Patch of Trouble

Fall to Pieces

Rest in Pieces

On Pins and Needles

Fit to be Tied

Embroidering the Truth

Knot a Clue

Quilt-Ridden

Needled to Death

A Notion to Murder

Crosspatch

Behind the Seams

Quilt Complex

A Southern Quilting Cozy Christmas

MEMPHIS BARBEQUE MYSTERIES in Order (Written as Riley Adams):

Delicious and Suspicious

Finger Lickin' Dead

Hickory Smoked Homicide

Rubbed Out

And a standalone "cozy zombie" novel: Race to Refuge, written as Liz Craig